They're out to get Pride . . .

Calls of congratulation came from all sides as Samantha, Ashleigh, Mike, and Charlie made their way to the winner's circle to see Pride. Mr. Townsend was already there looking incredibly pleased. Lavinia and Brad were with him. Samantha noticed Lavinia giving Ashleigh a look of such absolute dislike that Samantha momentarily shuddered. But fortunately Ashleigh hadn't noticed, and Samantha tried to put it out of her mind, too, as she took Pride's head and kissed him soundly on the nose.

"You were incredible!" she murmured, still feeling a little awed by his performance in the race. Pride huffed an excited breath as Jilly dismounted and removed the saddle to weigh in.

By the time Jilly returned to remount for the winner's photo, Lavinia and Brad had followed Mr. Townsend to Pride's side. Samantha wasn't surprised that they wanted to be in the photo, even if they were having a very difficult time looking pleased. What surprised her was the venom in Lavinia's voice as she muttered to Brad, "This won't happen again."

D0288212

Collect all the books in the
THOROUGHBRED series:

THOROUGHBRED Super Editions:

Ashleigh's Christmas Miracle
Ashleigh's Diary
Ashleigh's Hope
Samantha's Journey

ASHLEIGH'S
Thoroughbred Collection:

Star of Shadowbrook Farm
The Forgotten Filly
Battlecry Forever!

*coming soon

THOROUGHBRED

PRIDE'S CHALLENGE

JOANNA CAMPBELL

HarperPaperbacks

A Division of HarperCollins*Publishers*

If you purchased this book without a cover, you should be aware that this book is stolen property. It was reported as "unsold and destroyed" to the publisher and neither the author nor the publisher has received any payment for this "stripped book."

This is a work of fiction. The characters, incidents, and dialogues are products of the author's imagination and are not to be construed as real. Any resemblance to actual events or persons, living or dead, is entirely coincidental.

HarperPaperbacks   *A Division of* HarperCollins*Publishers*
10 East 53rd Street, New York, N.Y. 10022

Copyright © 1994 by Daniel Weiss Associates, Inc., and Joanna Campbell
Cover art copyright © 1994 Daniel Weiss Associates, Inc.

All rights reserved. No part of this book may be used or reproduced in any manner whatsoever without written permission of the publisher, except in the case of brief quotations embodied in critical articles and reviews. For information address Daniel Weiss Associates, Inc., 33 West 17th Street, New York, New York 10011.

Produced by Daniel Weiss Associates, Inc., 33 West 17th Street, New York, New York 10011.

First printing: May 1994

Printed in the United States of America

HarperPaperbacks and colophon are trademarks of HarperCollins*Publishers*

10

PRIDE'S CHALLENGE

"ALL RIGHT!" SAMANTHA MCLEAN SHOUTED AS SHE AND Wonder's Pride swept past the mile marker on the training oval at Whitebrook Farm. Samantha lifted her slim, five-foot-four frame out of Pride's saddle and raised a fist in triumph. Her red hair streamed out from beneath her helmet. At sixteen, Samantha had been exercise riding high-strung and powerful Thoroughbreds for three years. She knew without seeing a stopwatch that the fractions they had set had been perfect. Charlie Burke, Pride's crusty old trainer, would be pleased, and so would his half-owner, Ashleigh Griffen.

Samantha slowed the big chestnut horse and briskly patted his neck. "Way to go, Pride!" she praised excitedly. "You're back in top form!" Pride bobbed his elegant head in acknowledgment.

It was amazing how well Pride had rebounded after the injury he'd sustained in the Breeders' Cup

Classic the previous autumn. He had stumbled coming out of the starting gate, catching his foreleg with his rear hoof. But the worst damage had been done when Pride had refused to stop running. Even Ashleigh, his jockey at the time, had been fooled into thinking Pride was okay—until Pride had come to a limping halt in the stretch, blood pouring from a gash on his foreleg. His leg had required surgery, and no one had known then if Pride would ever race again. It had been one of the worst moments in Samantha's life. Yet now, in early June, Pride *was* ready to race.

As Samantha turned Pride to head off the track, she saw that Ashleigh and Charlie weren't the only ones watching the workout. Standing at the rail were Brad Townsend and his new bride, Lavinia. They were an extraordinarily attractive couple—perfectly dressed, with Brad's dark good looks contrasting with Lavinia's gleaming blond hair. But Samantha cringed to see them. Brad's father was half-owner of Pride and owner of Townsend Acres, the prestigious farm where Pride had been bred and raised. Samantha respected Clay Townsend. She did not respect his son. From past experience she knew that when Brad appeared on the scene, trouble usually followed.

Samantha felt some of her exhilaration from the successful workout fade as she rode off the track in the pale early-morning sunlight. She saw the frowns on Ashleigh and Charlie's faces and knew they were thinking the same thing she was—what were Brad and Lavinia doing here?

Charlie ignored the two visitors as Samantha rode up and prepared to dismount. His old blue eyes carefully scrutinized Pride; then he squinted up at Samantha. "You did that last half-mile just the way I wanted," he said. He pushed back his floppy hat and knelt to remove the protective bandages on Pride's forelegs and make a careful examination. He nodded in satisfaction. "His leg looks good. I'd say he's ready for the Nassau County this weekend."

Ashleigh had come to Pride's side, too, and lovingly patted his neck. "You're back in shape, boy," she said. "And you know it, don't you?" Pride nudged her shoulder with his nose.

Lavinia's haughty voice pierced the air as she spoke to Brad. "I don't know how they can be so sure of that. After that injury, how *could* he come back one hundred percent? Just because he puts in a few good workouts doesn't mean he's fit. I can't understand why you and your father are even considering racing him again—especially now that we have Lord Ainsley."

Samantha's blood boiled just listening. Who was Lavinia to talk? She had absolutely *no* experience in training or racing, yet since she had married Brad in April, Lavinia had suddenly become an expert on the Thoroughbred industry.

"It's true he'd make more money for us at stud," Brad answered, "but my father wants to keep racing him. I wouldn't worry, though. Pride doesn't stand a chance against Lord Ainsley in the Nassau."

Lavinia smiled at Brad's words. She had bought Lord

Ainsley, a multimillion-dollar English Thoroughbred, for Brad as a wedding present, and so far Lord Ainsley was living up to his reputation and the Townsends' expectations. Two weeks before, he had won the Grade 1 Pimlico Special by an impressive margin. Lavinia hadn't stopped gloating.

"I don't know why your father doesn't let *you* make more of the decisions," Lavinia said. "If he's so intent on racing Pride, there are other, smaller races."

Ashleigh angrily cut into their conversation. "Maybe you've forgotten, Lavinia," she said, "but I happen to be half-owner of Pride. I have a say in all the decisions, and Mr. Townsend and I agree. Pride is ready to race again, and you can be darn sure he's going to give your horse a run for the money."

Lavinia looked over at Ashleigh. "Pride may have won two legs of the Triple Crown last year," she said, "but I don't think much of the horses he beat."

"You were happy enough to pose in the winner's circle with him," Ashleigh snapped.

"He was running under Townsend Acres' colors. Of course we'd be there."

"Even if you had absolutely nothing to do with his success?"

"And that was *last* year," Lavinia continued arrogantly. "You know as well as we do that Pride is past his prime. The only reason you're so determined to keep him competing is because you haven't got another decent horse *on* this place. You're expecting us to waste our money on entry fees for a horse that doesn't stand a chance."

4

"You don't know what you're talking about," Ashleigh said. "You have absolutely no experience training. You wouldn't know how to recognize a horse's potential if you fell over it. You're the last one qualified to make any judgments!"

Lavinia narrowed her blue eyes as she glared at Ashleigh. "You've just been fortunate that my father-in-law has a soft spot for you. It's disgusting the way he lets you manipulate him."

"If there's any manipulation going on, you're the one who's doing it," Ashleigh retorted. "And when you're at Whitebrook, you can keep your uninformed comments to yourself!"

"You owe Lavinia an apology," Brad said angrily to Ashleigh.

"Oh? She's the one throwing around the insults, not me. I don't come over to Townsend Acres and tell you how to run your training operation."

"It's a little different in this case, isn't it?" Brad said. "We do own half of Pride."

"Your *father* does—not you!"

Lavinia's features were pinched with anger. "I've had enough of this," she said to Brad. "Let's get out of here."

"Yes, do that," Ashleigh said. She stared after them as they strode off toward Brad's Ferrari. For a long moment Ashleigh stood with hands on her hips, taking deep breaths to control her anger. "I don't believe her," Ashleigh muttered. "Who does she think she is?"

Not until Brad had turned the Ferarri and roared up the drive did Ashleigh seem to calm down a little.

5

She let out a long breath. "I probably shouldn't have said all that."

"She deserved it!" Samantha cried. "She's such a complete snob—and how *dare* she tell you what's good or bad for Pride? How dare Brad say anything either!" Samantha remembered too well the problems the Townsends had caused the year before when Brad had tried to interfere with Pride's training and race schedule. He'd pressured his normally reasonable father into overracing the colt, and when Pride had started losing races due to the unwarranted pressure, the Townsends had removed Charlie as trainer and Ashleigh as jockey. Pride had nearly been ruined, and it had taken weeks of rest and tender loving care before Samantha, Ashleigh, and Charlie had been able to bring Pride back to form. Mr. Townsend had admitted he'd made a mistake by interfering. Brad never had. "Lavinia was pretty angry at what you said, though," Samantha added.

"And not likely to forget real quick," Charlie said. "She may not know anything about training Thoroughbreds, but she sure seems to be leading the Townsend kid around with a nose ring. And I don't care what kind of family she grew up with," he added to Ashleigh. "It doesn't cut with me."

Samantha frowned, remembering what Ashleigh had learned about Lavinia from the wife of a fellow Lexington breeder. The breeder's wife had known Lavinia's family for years. She told Ashleigh that Lavinia had grown up in Virginia, the only child of the very wealthy Hotchkins-Ross family, but she hadn't had an easy or happy childhood. Her socialite mother had blatantly ignored her and was rarely at home. Lavinia's father had tried to make up for his wife's neglect and had pampered Lavinia, providing her with everything money could buy and trying to shield her from further disappointment. The result was that Lavinia had reached her twenties with a very high opinion of herself, never questioning that if she wanted something, she would get it. "Of course," the woman had told Ashleigh, "the one thing she didn't get was her mother's love."

"Well, I sure don't feel sorry for her either," Samantha told Charlie. "Though I suppose she couldn't help the way she was brought up. But other people have had it rough. That's no excuse for being so obnoxious."

"I've also heard she's poured plenty of money into Townsend Acres," Ashleigh said. "That probably makes her feel she's got a say in the way things are run over there. You know how Townsend Acres was hurting for money a year ago."

Charlie straightened his hat. "It's water over the dam now. At least Clay Townsend has more sense than to listen to her. And she was right about one thing. Pride may be training well, but there's no guarantee how a horse will come back after an injury and long layoff. We could get beaten. Keep that in mind."

"Charlie!" Samantha cried. "You saw how he worked today. And he felt wonderful, too. He was on the bit the whole time and just wanted to go."

"Yup, but like I said, there're no guarantees. Lord

Ainsley's not going to be an easy horse to beat. Don't forget, he was last year's English champion, and he walked all over the field in the Pimlico Special. Much as I hate to say it, that little snip may be proved right."

"No way!" Samantha said, looking at Pride and feeling her heart swell again. He breathed softly into her palm as she reached up to rub his velvet nose. "That won't happen, will it, boy?" But Charlie's words left Samantha feeling uneasy. What if they did lose to Lord Ainsley? What if Pride put in a clunker? Then what would Lavinia and Brad have to say?

AFTER LEN, WHITEBROOK'S STABLE MANAGER, HAD COL-
lected Pride to cool him out, Ashleigh left for the stable office to talk to her fiancé, Mike Reese, co-owner
of the farm. Samantha looked up the farm drive and
saw her boyfriend, Tor Nelson, approaching in his
car. She hurried over to meet him.

Tor's blond hair shone in the sunlight as he strode
up to Samantha with a smile on his face. He gave her
a quick hug. "So how did Pride's workout go?" he
asked.

"He couldn't have done better," Samantha said, returning his smile, "except that Brad and Lavinia
showed up and tried to stick in their two cents." She
explained what had happened.

"I wouldn't let Lavinia's opinions worry you,"
Tor said.

"No, except it makes me angry that she and Brad
have to come over here and upset Ashleigh. She's

9

been so up since she graduated from college last month—she's excited about Pride's comeback and her wedding next month."

"Well, look at the bright side," Tor said. "Even if Lavinia and Brad are being a pain, overall, things are looking up. Pride is definitely ready to return to the races, and Sierra's coming along the way we want."

"Right!" Samantha agreed more cheerfully. "Let's go get him." They headed toward the barn where Sierra was stabled. Together they were retraining the three-year-old colt, who had failed dismally in his training as a flat racer. A few months before Mike had been ready to sell the headstrong horse, but Tor and Samantha had discovered that Sierra had other talents—he could jump! They had convinced Mike to let them work with the colt. Sierra had taken to steeplechasing like he was born to it, but not until he had run a fast-closing second in his first 'chase in April had Mike relented and decided to keep him.

"We'll need to get a good work from Sierra over the fences today since you'll be going to New York on Friday for Pride's race," Tor said. "I won't be able to work him again until you get back."

As they headed across the stable yard they were surrounded by the white-fenced, grassy paddocks of Whitebrook. Most contained grazing Thoroughbreds. All of them were sleek and beautiful animals. Samantha's father, Ian McLean, was head trainer on the farm and looked after the horses that were boarded at Whitebrook for training. Samantha's mother had been killed in a tragic riding accident four years before, and Samantha and her father lived alone in one of the immaculate cottages on the property. Charlie and Len shared the other cottage, and Mike and his father lived in the small main house across the stable yard.

"I know," Samantha said, and glanced at the plaster cast that encased Tor's left forearm. "Did you go to the doctor yesterday?" she asked.

Tor smiled. "Good news. He said I should be able to ride again in a couple of weeks!"

"All right! Then you'll definitely be able to ride Sierra in the 'chase at Atlantic City!"

"Looks like it, but I don't know why you sound so relieved. You did a great job riding him at Lexington," Tor said.

"And you know I was scared out of my mind. I wouldn't have had the courage to do it if you hadn't broken your arm."

"You're better than you think you are, Sammy. And you're getting better all the time."

Samantha looked up and smiled. "Thanks. I have a great teacher, but I have a long way to go before I'm as good as you."

Tor laughed. "Not that I've had much practice lately with this thing!" He lifted his bad arm.

"But as soon as the cast's off you can start working Top Hat again," Samantha said.

"Yeah, though I don't know if we'll be ready for any shows this summer. My father's been taking Top Hat over the jumps, but it's too late to get both of us in top form. At least my college classes are

11

over for the semester, so I'll have more time."

As they stepped into the barn where Sierra and Pride were stabled, Sidney, one of the three stable cats, came trotting down the aisle toward them. He was nearly grown but still kittenish. He had very distinctive markings, including a black band that ran down his face, around his eyes, and over his nose and chin like a mask. Sidney arched his back and leaped the last few steps, then wound his black-and-white body around Samantha's ankles. She reached down to pat him. "Waiting for Pride to get back, Sid?" she asked the purring animal. The young cat and horse had formed a special bond. Sidney was usually found somewhere near Pride's stall and frequently curled up on the big chestnut's back for a snooze. "He'll be here soon," Samantha said. The cat jumped up onto one of the stall partitions as Samantha and Tor continued down the aisle.

Sierra was in one of the end stalls, and he already had his head over the door watching them approach. He whinnied impatiently, eager to be outside.

"Yeah, we're coming, monster," Samantha called affectionately to the colt. Sierra was known for his mischievous personality. He could be willful and never hesitated to take advantage of his rider if he thought he could get away with it, but Samantha loved him anyway. She was thrilled that he was finally showing the talent she had always believed he had.

Tor collected Sierra's tack, and Samantha led Sierra out into the aisle and fastened a set of crossties to his halter. Sierra's liver-chestnut coat gleamed from the careful grooming Len had given him. Len loved the ornery colt as much as Samantha did.

They soon had Sierra tacked up. Samantha was unclipping the crossties when Mike came down the aisle toward them, walking with a middle-aged man. Thoroughbred owners frequently stopped by the farm, interested in having their horses boarded and trained at Whitebrook. Mike's blond head was tilted thoughtfully as he listened to something the other man was saying. As they approached, Samantha overheard part of their conversation. "Since I was going to be in the area anyway," the man said to Mike, "I thought it wouldn't hurt to stop by and take a look at him. And maybe convince you to change your mind."

"I don't think that's going to happen," Mike replied. "What I said to you on the phone still goes. I've decided to hold on to him. But you're free to have a look at him. Here he is." Mike motioned to Sierra. "Hi, guys," he added with a smile to Samantha and Tor.

The other man's eyes brightened with interest as his gaze rested on Sierra. Samantha frowned.

Sierra started prancing in place as if he knew he was the object of attention.

The man obviously was impressed. "*Very* handsome animal," he said, walking around the colt. "Nice breadth of chest, good straight leg, strong hindquarters, intelligent eyes."

"Oh, he's no dummy," Mike answered. "Unfortunately in the past, he used that intelligence to outsmart us. But we've found the trick to turn him around, I think. He's taken to steeplechasing like he was bred for it. By the way, let me introduce you to the two people who worked the magic. Fred, Samantha McLean and Tor Nelson. Sammy and Tor, Fred Walters, who runs Oakhill Stud in Florida and was interested in buying Sierra."

Fred Walters nodded a greeting. "Pleased to meet you." He continued studying Sierra. "I'm glad you're making progress with him, but I'm still set on having him. I've liked his bloodlines all along, and I have some well-bred mares I'd like to cross with him." He looked back to Mike. "Now that I've seen him, I'm even more convinced. I'll give you two hundred and fifty thousand for him."

Samantha gasped and heard Tor's own indrawn breath. She could see that Mike had been thrown totally off guard. The offer was more than *twice* what Mike could have reasonably expected for Sierra!

Mike frowned. "That's pretty generous."

"I'm willing to pay generously for a horse I really want."

For agonizing seconds, Mike was silent—as if he were actually considering the offer. *Say you're not interested*, Samantha thought desperately. But she knew how tempting the offer had to be to Mike. Stallions that were unproven on the track weren't that much in demand for stud, even if they had far more exceptional bloodlines than Sierra's. Offers like Fred Walters's didn't come along every day. Although Sierra was showing his potential as a steeplechaser, steeplechase purses weren't that big. He would have

14

to win a lot of 'chases to earn a quarter of a million dollars.

"I have to admit you've kind of blown me away," Mike said. "I can't sniff at an offer like that. The farm always needs the cash flow."

"Then we have a deal," Fred Walters said happily, extending his hand.

Samantha's heart dropped to her feet. After all she and Tor had been through retraining Sierra and proving his ability to Mike, Mike was going to sell him anyway! Samantha stared at Mike and thought of the plans and dreams she and Tor had for the three-year-old colt.

But Mike hadn't yet taken Walters's hand to shake in agreement to the sale. Instead he glanced in Samantha and Tor's direction, then turned and let his gaze rest on Sierra.

Suddenly Sierra drew his teeth back from his lips and snaked his head forward in the direction of Fred Walters's arm. Fortunately the Florida breeder reacted quickly and stepped out of reach before Sierra's strong square teeth closed on his skin. Samantha almost smiled as Sierra gave an unremorseful whinny. She liked to think that Sierra was deliberately showing his worst side to his prospective buyer.

"So he's a nipper," Fred Walters said, though he didn't sound deterred.

"He has a regular bag of tricks," Mike answered, still thoughtfully studying Sierra.

"Well, that's certainly not a problem," Walters said. "My handlers are all experienced and have dealt with some pretty mean-tempered stallions."

"He's not mean!" Samantha burst out.

Walters looked over to her. "I didn't say he was. Anyway, all that matters to me is that he's friendly toward the mares. So, we have a deal?" he added to Mike. "I've got a certified check with me, and I can get a van over to pick him up this afternoon."

Samantha glanced over to Tor and saw he looked as sick as she felt. All their work, down the tubes! And it wasn't just the work—she *cared* about Sierra. She didn't want him shipped off to some strange farm where she'd never see him again! Obviously Fred Walters wanted to own Sierra, not just have breeding rights to him when he was retired.

Finally Mike spoke. "I hate to disappoint you, Fred, and I do appreciate how generous your offer is, but I want to hold on to him."

Samantha felt her knees go weak with relief. Tor reached over to take her hand and give it a quick squeeze.

Fred Walters's eyes widened in disbelief. He spoke quickly to Mike. "But I've just made you an incredible offer! I don't know of anyone who would match it."

"Probably no one would, and like I said, I appreciate the offer," Mike answered, "but I've decided I like this guy too much to sell him."

"I think you're making a big mistake," Walters said. "What are a few steeplechase purses going to earn you? And there's no guarantee he'll even win."

"I know, but I'd like to give him the opportunity," Mike said. "Look, if I ever change my mind and decide to sell him, you'll have first option, if you're still interested."

For a moment Walters frowned, then he shrugged. "Guess I'll have to make do with that, though I can't guarantee my offer would be so high—the market changes."

"I understand," Mike said. "Listen, as long as you're here, we do have a couple of other horses I am interested in selling. They don't have Sierra's bloodlines, but they're good stock. Maybe you'd like to see them."

Walters, obviously disappointed, took one last look at Sierra, then followed Mike down the aisle.

Samantha and Tor turned and gave each other a spontaneous hug. "I was so afraid!" Samantha cried. "It was so much money to offer."

"I know," Tor agreed. "I almost can't believe Mike turned it down—but boy, am I glad!"

Fifteen minutes later Samantha had finished warming up Sierra on the inner turf course of the training oval. Around the course Tor had positioned eight four-foot-high, hedgelike jumps. After the shock of Fred Walters's offer, Samantha had had a little trouble concentrating, but her mind was firmly on business now.

"He's ready to go," she said to Tor. "Do you want me to take him around twice, or do you think that would be too much?" Since they were heading Sierra toward a much more difficult and competitive race than his first steeplechase, their object was to keep Sierra in the best physical condition and to polish his technique over the jumps. The course he would have to jump at the Atlantic City racetrack would be two-and-an-eighth miles long, with sixteen fences he and Tor would have to get over cleanly. They'd also have to have enough speed between and over the fences to win the race. Samantha and Tor had been alternating Sierra's training with workouts over the jumps and long, slow gallops on the flat to build up his stamina. They didn't want to overwork him, though. They still had five weeks before his race.

"Once is enough for today," Tor told her.

Samantha nodded and prepared herself, adjusting her grip on the reins and her seat in the saddle. She began circling Sierra at a canter and saw Mike, Fred Walters, and Len walk to the rail to watch the workout. *Darn,* she thought. *Now we'll really have to put in a perfect round.* She forced herself to concentrate, and as they came up to the marker pole she squeezed with her legs, gave Sierra rein, and clucked to him.

Sierra bounded forward toward the first fence, which was a little less than an eighth of a mile up the track. Samantha's head was up, her eyes focused forward on the fence as they rapidly approached. She headed Sierra toward the center of the fence, though in an actual steeplechase horse and rider didn't always have a choice about where they jumped. There would be other horses and riders trying to get over the fence, too, and the object would be to avoid a collision.

Without seeming to need any guidance from Samantha, Sierra gathered his hindquarters at the perfect takeoff point, lifted, and soared over the fence. Samantha stretched with him, arms extended along his neck, heels well down in her stirrups. Then they were landing, and Sierra was bounding off toward the next fence.

On they went around the course, Samantha holding the big colt to a moderate gallop. This training session wasn't the time to press Sierra's pace between the fences. They were trying to hone his jumping technique. Closer to race time, they would work on both speed and technique.

As usual Sierra wanted to increase the pace on his own, but Samantha had her fingers tight on the reins. They worked their way down the backstretch and around the turn. *We're doing well,* Samantha thought. *Two more fences.*

They came off the turn and cleared the second-to-last fence.

"We'd better finish this in style, Sierra," Samantha warned, conscious of the men standing opposite the last fence. Sierra was striding energetically toward the obstacle. Samantha mentally counted strides, preparing to squeeze with her legs and give rein—not that Sierra usually needed much encouragement to jump. Sierra seemed to be intent on impressing the spectators, too. He seemed to have springs on his heels as he gathered himself and flew over the final fence. As they landed, Samantha knew it was their best jump yet. She smiled to herself as she headed Sierra down the last stretch of track toward the marker pole. She couldn't stop herself from glancing over to Tor and the others to see their reactions. In

19

that same instant Sierra exploded beneath her, lunging forward into a mad gallop.

Samantha groaned. She had unconsciously relaxed, and Sierra had sensed it. She should have known better! He'd pulled the same stunt on her before, taking her on a mad and terrifying gallop through the woods.

She collected what she could of the reins and her wits, but Sierra was out to have a little fun now. He pounded toward the first fence of the second circuit, ignoring her tug on the reins as she tried to stop him. Samantha knew his galloping strides were bringing them up to the fence much too quickly. They'd never meet the fence right. Sierra would probably get them over, but it wouldn't be a beautiful sight to see.

Samantha prepared herself as best she could and tried to adjust Sierra's stride. He wanted no part of it. Samantha knew as he gathered for the fence that they were much too close. They were going to pop over the jump, and the landing was going to be uncomfortable. As Sierra lifted, she thrust her heels down in the stirrups and gathered handfuls of mane with the reins. Still, the jolt of their unbalanced landing threw her far up on Sierra's neck. Her heels popped up and she lost the stirrups. As Sierra's rear feet touched the ground, his head came up, connecting with Samantha's nose and sending stars swimming before her eyes. She felt herself sliding out of the saddle and falling to the ground. She landed on her back as Sierra galloped on, riderless.

For several seconds she lay stunned. She reached up her hand to her nose. It wasn't bleeding, but it throbbed painfully. As she lifted herself on her elbows, Tor raced up. Mike and Len were right behind him.

"Are you all right?" Tor asked worriedly.

"I think so. I banged my nose pretty bad," Samantha said, shaking her head quickly to clear it. "It was my fault. I relaxed coming down the stretch, and he took off. We met this fence all wrong."

Tor put a hand under her elbow and helped her stand. "I saw," he said.

Now that she was on her feet, Samantha looked around for Sierra. He was merrily jumping the rest of the course without a rider.

As Len set off to intercept and catch the colt, Fred Walters walked over and chuckled dryly. "So you really think you're going to make something out of him? I'd say he has a mind of his own."

"He has his flaws," Mike admitted, "but you saw the way he was jumping. He has talent. Are you sure you're all right, Sammy?" he added with concern.

"Fine—just a little angry at myself."

"Well, my offer stands," Walters said to Mike. "You might get tired of him tossing jockeys."

Len approached them, leading an unrepentant Sierra by the reins. The colt came willingly enough now that he'd worked off his high spirits.

Len looked at Samantha and shook his head. "He always seems to put on a show at the worst moment," the old man said.

"I know." Samantha only hoped Sierra's performance that day hadn't given Mike second thoughts about Walters's offer.

Fred Walters was preparing to leave. "Well, I wish you luck with training him," he said to Mike. "I think you're going to need it."

TOR DROVE SAMANTHA TO SCHOOL THAT MORNING. SHE arrived with just enough time to change her books at her locker. Her best friend, Yvonne Ortez, and the petite features editor of the school paper, Maureen O'Brien, were waiting at her locker. All three girls were finishing their junior year at Henry Clay High.

"You look like you're in a rush," Yvonne said as Samantha hurried up. Yvonne's dark eyes and her shining straight black hair were evidence of her Navajo-English-Spanish heritage.

"I am. The workouts took longer than I expected."

"And how did they go? Did Pride do all right?" Maureen asked with concern. Both girls knew how important that morning's workout had been.

Samantha filled the two of them in on all the details, including Lavinia and Brad's visit. "Anyway," she added, "the good news is that Tor will definitely be able to ride at Atlantic City. The doctor said his arm is doing great."

"Then he can start riding Top Hat again soon," Yvonne said excitedly. "But I don't suppose they'll be ready for the big show in two weeks."

Samantha shook her head. "But *you* will be. Tor says you've been riding incredibly well. He thinks you'll get a blue ribbon." For the past two years Yvonne had been taking jumping lessons from Tor. She'd progressed so rapidly, she would be competing at the advanced level at the next show.

Yvonne beamed. "You're coming to the show, aren't you?"

"Are you kidding? I wouldn't miss it! I can finally get to meet this guy Gregg you keep talking about."

Yvonne's smile widened. "You'll like Gregg. He's nothing like Jay. Boy, am I glad I broke up with *him* last spring. I was definitely wasting my time."

"Could I come to the show, too?" Maureen asked eagerly. "I've never seen you jump."

"Sure," Yvonne said. "But I'll be a nervous wreck with all you guys watching."

"You'll forget about being nervous once you're out on the course," Samantha told her. "There's the warning bell."

"I'll see you at lunch," Maureen said before hurrying off. "I'll save a table if I get there first."

Samantha and Yvonne set off in the opposite direction. "The more I think about Brad and Lavinia coming to Whitebrook this morning," Samantha said, "the more nervous it makes me. It worries me, too."

"I know what you mean," Yvonne sympathized. "You and Ashleigh have already gone through so much because of Brad."

"Don't remind me," Samantha answered. "But I don't think they can start any more trouble before the Nassau, and I feel really good about Pride's chances. If you had seen the way he was working this morning—he's just amazing!"

Tor drove Samantha to the airport Friday afternoon, kissing her good-bye at the gate and wishing her luck. The day before Samantha had talked to Ashleigh, who was already at Belmont Park in New York with Charlie and Pride. Ashleigh had said everything was going fine. Samantha had sensed, though, that there was something Ashleigh wasn't telling her, and she was worried.

When Ashleigh picked her up at La Guardia Airport on Long Island, Samantha knew immediately that something was wrong. Ashleigh looked tense and tired and was obviously upset. As they drove to the Belmont track Ashleigh described the horrendous few days she'd just spent.

"I didn't want to say anything when I talked to you on the phone," Ashleigh said, "but Lavinia and Brad are doing everything to make my life miserable. They're always hanging around Pride's stall. Lavinia's acting like *she's* the owner of Townsend Acres. She's bad-mouthing me all over the track, telling people Pride's physically not ready to race—that I'm so desperate, I refuse to do what's best for the horse."

Samantha had turned to stare at Ashleigh. "How does Mr. Townsend let her get away with that kind of stuff? It's not true!"

"He hasn't been here," Ashleigh answered. "He stayed down at Townsend Acres and is only coming up tomorrow for the race. I get this scary feeling that he's giving Brad—and that means Lavinia, too—more and more control over the Townsend Acres operation."

That left Samantha with a very scary feeling as well. "What Lavinia's saying is only talk, though," she said. "When Pride gets out on the track, he'll show everyone Lavinia's all wrong."

"Oh, I know," Ashleigh agreed. "But she's got me so rattled, I'm starting to doubt myself, and there are people who believe her. She can be so charming when she wants to, and she's rolling in money. That impresses some people who should know better, and a lot of people don't realize how little she actually knows about training. When she's spouting off, I've seen Brad just stand there smiling, like he agrees with every word she's saying."

"*He's* got to know better than that!" Samantha exclaimed. "He's obnoxious, but he does know something about horses. He must know Pride *is* ready to race."

"Oh, I think Brad's enjoying the trouble Lavinia's starting. He didn't look very good last year after he tried interfering with Pride's training, especially when Pride started winning again after Charlie and I got him back. Brad would love to see me looking bad. I tell myself to ignore them—but it's getting to me.

26

Yesterday when I worked Pride on the track here, I couldn't do anything right. I was confusing and upsetting him. I've decided not to ride tomorrow—I can't jeopardize Pride's chances in the race. I've asked Jilly to ride."

Samantha knew Jilly Gordon well, but she felt stunned at Ashleigh's decision. Jilly was good and handled her mounts just as Samantha or Ashleigh would. She was the former jockey of Pride's dam, Ashleigh's Wonder, and had been riding for the season at Churchill Downs in Kentucky with her jockey husband, Craig Avery. Jilly would also be one of Ashleigh's bridesmaids, along with Samantha, Ashleigh's sister, Caroline, and Ashleigh's old friend, Linda March. "Did Jilly say yes?" Samantha asked.

Ashleigh nodded. "She and Craig are flying up from Louisville tonight. I think I've made the right decision—I have to do what's right for Pride. Charlie agrees. And Jilly knows Pride, since she rode him in his early training."

"I just feel so bad that Brad and Lavinia are making you this upset! Do they know you've changed jockeys? What did Mr. Townsend say?"

"I haven't said a word to Brad or Lavinia," Ashleigh answered. "As far as I'm concerned, it's none of their business. It's up to Mr. Townsend, and he said fine. I told him I wasn't feeling well. I suppose you could say that's true."

"I wonder what Brad and Lavinia will say when they find out."

"Brad, at least, will be happy I'm *not* riding.

Lavinia will probably try to twist it around so I look bad, but I don't care anymore. All that matters is that Pride has the best chance possible going into the race."

Ashleigh pulled into the immense Belmont backside, with its rows and rows of stabling barns.

Samantha was still trying to absorb all the bad news. "Is Pride all right, though?" she asked worriedly.

"Charlie and I are guarding him like hawks. I'm really glad now that we brought him up here only a few days ago. I'm trying real hard not to let him sense how upset I am. You know how he picks up on the feelings of the people around him."

"Maybe I should set up a cot by his stall tonight," Samantha suggested.

"No, you won't need to do that. Charlie will be close by, and barn security is tight. I can't see Lavinia or Brad stooping low enough to bother Pride during the night." But Ashleigh frowned as she parked the car.

Samantha knew her way around the Belmont backside from many previous visits. She and Ashleigh headed toward the row of stabling that Townsend Acres reserved on a regular basis. Even at that early-evening hour, the backside was bustling. Two very important races would be run the following day—the Belmont Stakes, which was the third jewel of the Triple Crown, and the Nassau County Handicap for older horses. Owners, trainers, grooms, and reporters moved around the lanes between the barns. Some horses were being walked, but most were secure in their stalls for the night.

28

Charlie was standing not far from Pride's stall, talking to Hank, the longtime head groom at Townsend Acres and Charlie's good friend. Pride had his elegant head over the stall door and whinnied happily when he saw Samantha approach. Samantha hurried up to the horse. She took his head in her hands and dropped a kiss on his velvet nose. "Hi there, big guy. I've missed you, even if you've only been gone a few days."

Pride affectionately nudged Samantha's shoulder with his nose, then rubbed the side of his head against her arm.

"He's as set for the race as he can be," Charlie said as he and Hank walked over. "Even if certain people aren't making life any easier around here."

Hank shook his head unhappily. "Charlie's sure right about that," he agreed, "but I guess Ashleigh's told you what's been going on with Brad and his wife."

Samantha nodded. "She has."

"I'm almost embarrassed to be working for them," Hank said. "Lavinia hasn't been making any friends among the staff at Townsend Acres either. She's been trying to boss everybody around. Clay Townsend will be here in the morning, thank heavens. Maybe he can straighten the two of them out."

"What do you think of Lord Ainsley?" Samantha asked.

"He's a good horse," Hank said. "There's no denying that. Ken Maddock is over the moon having a horse of Lord's caliber to train. It'll be a tight contest between him and Pride, but my money's on Pride. I've always thought Pride had that little something special. He's proved me right, too."

"And I think he will again," Samantha said loyally.

"A lot of others around here don't think like you do," Charlie said. "The fans love him, but the handicappers haven't forgotten that he hasn't raced in seven months. Don't expect miracles of this guy."

"What are you saying, Charlie?" Ashleigh cried. "That you think he's going to get beaten?"

"I'm not saying he's going to get beaten, but it would be foolish to get too cocky."

"It looks like it's going to be a two-horse race, anyway," Hank said. "Lord Ainsley beat a lot of the horses in this field in the Pimlico Special, and I don't see anything in the other starters to write home about."

"One of them could pull an upset," Charlie muttered. "It's happened."

Samantha knew Charlie was just being his usual pessimistic self. He considered it bad luck to have too high hopes coming up to a race. Generally, the more pessimistic he was beforehand, the better they did.

"Were Lavinia or Brad by while I was gone?" Ashleigh asked.

"Nope," Hank said. "I understand they're throwing a dinner party tonight. You'll see plenty of them tomorrow, though."

"Mmmm," Samantha murmured. The thought didn't make her happy.

*   *   *

30

Jilly and Craig showed up an hour later. Both of them were tired. They'd ridden at Churchill Downs earlier in the day, but they were glad to see everyone. "It's like old times," Jilly said, giving Ashleigh a hug. "I'd hug you, too, Charlie, but I know you wouldn't like it." She gave him a teasing but affectionate grin.

"So it sounds like you're having some trouble up here," Craig said to Ashleigh after he'd said his hellos.

"You've got it. I'm just relieved Jilly was free to ride."

"That's what friends are for," Craig said. "My agent even managed to get me a few rides tomorrow, too—not in the Nassau, though. I'll be cheering on Jilly and Pride."

"Let me see the big guy." Jilly walked toward Pride's stall. Pride stuck his head over the half-door and whickered. "It's been a long time, Pride," Jilly said, "but you're just as gorgeous as ever." She rubbed Pride's ears, and he huffed out an appreciative breath. "We'll show them tomorrow, won't we?" Jilly turned to Ashleigh and Charlie. "Do you have any special strategy for the race?" she asked.

"If Lord Ainsley's last two races are any indication," Ashleigh answered, "he likes to run just off the pace. That's how we were running Pride his last couple of times out, even though Pride doesn't like to be rated."

"The problem is that there's no early speed in the race," Charlie put in. "No one's going to be rushing after the lead, which means you'd be rating Pride through some pretty slow fractions. He'll like that even less. Ashleigh and I were thinking it might be best to just take him right to the front and hope he can take it gate to wire. That might catch Lord Ainsley's jockey by surprise, since he won't be expecting Pride to go to the front."

Jilly nodded thoughtfully and toyed with her long blond braid. "Before I came up, I watched a video of the Pimlico Special. If Lord Ainsley runs the same kind of race, I can expect him to start moving on the far turn and start pressuring us hard coming down the stretch."

"Right," Ashleigh said. "We're just hoping Pride will have plenty of steam left to hold him off. Pride's in top form. He's been training up to his race really well, but Lord Ainsley isn't going to let him run away with the honors. And you know how much Brad and Lavinia want to win this. Their jock, Le Blanc, is going in there to do battle."

"I was figuring on that," Jilly responded. "What I'm hoping is that Le Blanc is overconfident and underestimates the battle we're going to give him. Right, boy?" she said to Pride. "I don't think you're going to disappoint anyone."

It was totally mad in the barn area the next morning, with press and fans mobbing the stabling rows and trying to get a look at Pride. His return to the races against Lord Ainsley was gaining more attention than the Belmont Stakes. Samantha, Charlie, and Ashleigh had their hands full keeping the worst of the crowd away and keeping Pride calm despite all the commotion. But at least Brad and Lavinia hadn't shown their faces.

Samantha was smoothing a netted sheet over Pride's back when she heard Lavinia's distinctive voice outside the stall. She gritted her teeth, then turned as Lavinia approached with several of her friends. All of them were expensively and stylishly dressed. Samantha thought of her own dirt-smudged shorts and T-shirt, and she knew strands of her long red hair were coming loose from her ponytail.

Lavinia strode right up to the stall. She barely looked at Samantha. "Take him out and walk him around," she told Samantha. "My friends want to have a look at him."

"He's not going anywhere," Samantha said. "I just got him settled and I'm not disturbing him."

"Don't be ridiculous. Walking him around for a few minutes isn't going to disturb him." Lavinia turned her back on Samantha as if she expected her orders to be instantly carried out. She spoke sweetly to her friends. "Of course, we don't really think he has a chance of beating Lord Ainsley, especially after that injury he had in the fall, but he did nearly win the Triple Crown for us last year."

Samantha was furious. Pride was not reacting well to the visitors outside his stall either. He stomped uneasily. "He stays where he is, Lavinia," she said tightly.

Lavinia spun around and stared disbelievingly at Samantha. "Since when does a groom tell me what I can or cannot do with my own horse? I said take him out."

Samantha looked the older girl straight in the eye. "He's not *your* horse, and I don't take orders from you, Lavinia. I take orders from Charlie and Ashleigh."

An angry flush rose up Lavinia's cheeks. "He's a Townsend Acres horse, which gives me more than a little to say. I'll take him out myself. Give me the lead shank."

"No. He's not leaving the stall." *Especially in* your *hands,* Samantha added silently.

Suddenly Charlie's barking tones cut through the air. "What's going on here?" he said sharply. The old man stomped up.

"I think it's time you found another groom," Lavinia said. "*She's* refused to take Pride out, so I'm taking him out myself. I want my friends to have a good look at him."

"Sammy's following my instructions. Pride stays where he is," Charlie said. "Your friends can get a good enough look at him in the walking ring before the race."

"All this overprotectiveness is ridiculous," Lavinia snapped. "What's the harm in taking him out of his stall for a few minutes?"

"You been taking Lord Ainsley out and showing him off to all the gawkers?" Charlie asked.

"That's different."

"How? Far as I know, they're both running in the same race. You think it's okay to upset Pride here, but not your horse?"

"Pride doesn't stand a chance of winning anyway," Lavinia said.

34

For an instant a wizened smile flickered on Charlie's lips, then he said sharply, "Like I said, your friends can gawk at him all they want in the walking ring. For now he stays right where he is." He turned to Samantha. "If he's set, you can close the top door, Sammy. Let him take a snooze if he wants."

Samantha nodded, giving Pride a last pat. She was so angry, she was shaking. "They're going, boy. They won't be bothering you." Pride snorted softly into Samantha's hand.

Lavinia had turned to her friends. "How ridiculous—after this race, he'll probably be retired to stud anyway. Let's find Brad. You're all invited to have lunch with us in the clubhouse." Lavinia and her friends sauntered off.

Samantha let herself out of the stall and closed both halves of the door behind her.

Charlie pushed back his floppy felt hat. His blue eyes were glittering dangerously. "I'll have to have a word with Clay Townsend when he arrives. This is getting totally out of hand."

"Do you think it will do any good?" Samantha asked. "Lavinia seems to be getting exactly what she wants."

"We'll see," Charlie said. "Anyway, I think you and I ought to hang close to Pride's stall until it's time for the race."

4

SAMANTHA HEARD AN APPRECIATIVE, EXCITED MURMUR rise in the crowd surrounding the saddling paddock and walking ring as she and Charlie led Pride in with the rest of the field for the Nassau County Handicap. Pride's copper coat gleamed under the green-and-gold Townsend Acres sheet over his back. His head was up, and his ears pricked in response to the admiration from the crowd.

Lavinia and Brad were very visible at the far side of the saddling paddock. Samantha saw them and Clay Townsend talking to several reporters. Charlie had spoken to Mr. Townsend early that afternoon, and Mr. Townsend had said he'd have a word with Lavinia. But Samantha noticed with disgust that Lavinia looked as self-assured as ever. Whatever Mr. Townsend had said to her couldn't have been very severe.

Samantha glanced across the paddock to Lord Ainsley, who was being led in by Hank and Ken

Maddock, the head trainer at Townsend Acres. She had to admit that the big, dark bay colt looked superb. His ears were pricked alertly, and there was an energetic bounce in his step. His muscles rippled under the Townsend Acres sheet he also wore. Since Lord Ainsley and Pride were running for the same stable, they would go into the race as an entry—Lord Ainsley would wear the number 1 saddlecloth; Pride number 1A. They would be bet as an entry, too, meaning the odds on one would be the same as the odds on the other, although there had been plenty of speculation around the backside about who was the better horse. Pride seemed to be the sentimental favorite among racegoers, but a lot of people were concerned about how he would perform after his injury and long layoff. Of course, Lavinia and Brad's negative comments fueled that uncertainty. Samantha didn't care whether people bet on Pride or not. She knew he'd demonstrate every ounce of the heart and courage that had made him great.

She glanced back to the Townsends. Mr. Townsend was staring across to the two horses representing his stable. Samantha wondered what he was thinking. Did his loyalties lie with Pride, whom he'd bred on Townsend Acres? Or did he have private doubts, too, that Pride could win? No matter which horse won, Townsend Acres would benefit.

Ashleigh was waiting at Pride's saddling box. Her face was pale but grimly intent, and Samantha felt even angrier at Lavinia and Brad. This should be a happy time for Ashleigh. Pride was returning to the races, and Ashleigh's wedding day was approaching. Ashleigh should be smiling, not frowning with worry.

"Well, *he* looks great," Ashleigh said as she removed the sheet from Pride's back and folded it. She glanced over to the next box, where Ken Maddock was preparing to tack up Lord Ainsley. "So does the competition."

Samantha saw Brad and Lavinia start walking toward Lord Ainsley's box. "Here they come," she said under her breath. Ashleigh busied herself readying Pride's tack, but Brad and Lavinia didn't even look their way as they strode past. A moment later Mr. Townsend approached Pride's box.

"So what do you think, Charlie?" he said when he reached the old trainer's side. "You're sure he's ready to race today?"

"He's ready to go—as on his toes as he can be."

Mr. Townsend's expression was thoughtful. "I'd love to see him win it," he said.

Samantha gave Mr. Townsend a look of pleased surprise. So his loyalties *were* with Pride.

"Though I'm feeling kind of torn. I don't want to see my son disappointed either. Maybe Brad was right when he suggested we not race the two horses against each other." He frowned. "Too late now. I know Pride will give it his best shot, no matter what the outcome. How are you feeling, Ashleigh?" he asked with concern.

"Better, thanks, Mr. Townsend, but I think I made the right choice in asking Jilly to ride."

"She's a superb jockey. I have no qualms there."

Charlie, under the watchful eye of an official, had finished tacking Pride. Pride displayed his usual good manners, standing quietly, but Samantha knew he was excited at the prospect of racing and was raring to go. She glanced over and saw Lord Ainsley was equally collected, although one of the horses farther down the row of boxes was acting up.

"Get him out there and walk him around, Sammy," Charlie said as he gave Pride's shoulder a last pat. Samantha took a firmer grip on the lead shank and led Pride forward. As they started circling the walking ring, Samantha heard the admiring calls from the crowd and felt the dozens of eyes watching her and Pride's progress. "Great to see him back!" someone cried. "He's looking good!" another voice called.

There was no question that Pride did present a magnificent sight, but Samantha noticed that Lord Ainsley was getting plenty of attention, too.

"You can beat him, boy," Samantha whispered to Pride. "Maybe he's a good horse, but you're better." Samantha saw Lavinia and Brad smiling confidently as they watched their horse circle the ring. She hoped neither of them would have reason to smile when the race was over.

A few minutes later the jockeys entered the ring. Samantha stopped Pride as Charlie, Ashleigh, and Jilly approached. Jilly looked professional and confident in her silks. She and Craig had each ridden winners earlier in the day, and Jilly obviously wasn't letting anything rattle her. Samantha decided that Ashleigh had done the right thing in getting Jilly to ride.

"I don't think you need any more instructions from me or Ashleigh," Charlie said as he gave Jilly a leg into the saddle.

"Nope. I'm set, though I think you'd like to know that Le Blanc was sounding superconfident in the jocks' rooms. I think he's going to underestimate us."

At that, Ashleigh finally smiled.

"Just don't underestimate them," Charlie told Jilly.

"I definitely won't make that mistake."

"Well, good luck," Charlie added gruffly as Samantha led Pride and Jilly off for another circle of the walking ring.

Samantha trained her binoculars on the starting gate as the field finished their warm-up and started to load. Although Pride wore the 1A saddlecloth, he'd drawn the fourth post position—not bad, but Jilly would have to get him out fast and around the inside horses if they were going to run on the lead. Lord Ainsley was in the two slot.

As usual, Pride went in smoothly and stood at attention as the rest of the field loaded. Lord Ainsley was also standing quietly alert. All the horses were in. A tense second passed, then the gates opened. Eight horses surged onto the track. Samantha was thrilled to see that Pride broke sharply. In two bounding strides, he'd taken the lead. Jilly angled him in along the rail. One of the long shots in the field, Orbital, settled into second, with Lord Ainsley tucked just behind him in third, the place he liked to be early in the race.

Pride continued leading the field into the first turn. Jilly was holding him to a length lead with a firm grip on the reins. Samantha knew Jilly was trying to keep the pace moderate so Pride would have something left when Lord Ainsley challenged him in the stretch.

"That's it, Jilly," Ashleigh murmured. "You're doing great."

Samantha glanced over and saw that Ashleigh was perched at the edge of her seat, hunched forward as if she were in the saddle herself.

"They're entering the backstretch," the announcer called. "Wonder's Pride still in the lead. They're letting him set moderate fractions, twenty-four for the quarter, forty-six and change for the half, but Jilly Gordon hasn't asked him for run yet. Lord Ainsley is still in third, followed by Phone Line, Mari's Pleasure. The rest of the field are way back. They're approaching the far turn, and now Le Blanc is starting to move the English horse. They're edging up outside of Orbital. Jilly Gordon is sitting cool on Wonder's Pride. Lord Ainsley is definitely on the move. As they go into the far turn, he shoots past Orbital!"

Samantha saw Jilly glance back under her arm. Lord Ainsley was coming fast, but Pride was galloping strongly. She knew he had something left.

"Now!" Ashleigh cried as Pride approached the top of the stretch, with Lord Ainsley just off his flank and bearing down. "Let him out! All right!" she shouted hoarsely. Pride switched leads, and as Jilly gave rein he moved effortlessly into another gear. It was amazing to watch—even to Samantha, who had ridden him so often and knew what he was capable of. He started drawing away from Lord Ainsley, increasing his lead to a length.

"And *down* the stretch they come!" shrieked the announcer. "The two-horse race we've been expecting! Wonder's Pride, without any urging from Jilly Gordon, has the lead by a length. But Lord Ainsley has more left, too! He's coming at Wonder's Pride with a vengeance. They're at the sixteenth pole with only half a length dividing them. Now Lord Ainsley is up on Wonder's Pride's flank, who's in tight quarters along the rail. Le Blanc goes to a left-handed whip on Lord Ainsley. Jilly Gordon is still hand-riding the big chestnut Derby winner. And he's not finished! He's increasing his lead again! He's *full* of run! He's going to try to take it wire to wire. Lord Ainsley is not going to catch him. And he's under the wire! Wonder's Pride the winner by a length and a half! He did the last quarter in an amazing twenty-two seconds! Unbelievable. An incredible return for Wonder's Pride!"

The crowd was roaring its approval. Samantha's ears echoed from the din. She and Ashleigh exchanged a fierce, victorious hug. On the track Jilly had her fist raised in victory. Even from the distance Samantha could see the beaming smile on Jilly's face. She knew two people in the Townsend camp who wouldn't be smiling, though.

Lavinia looked ready to kill when she entered the winner's circle. Brad didn't look any happier. In contrast, Mr. Townsend seemed delighted.

"Why don't Brad and Lavinia just stay away?" Samantha muttered to Ashleigh as they stood at Pride's head while Jilly dismounted to weigh in.

"They'd never do that," Ashleigh answered. "They'll grab whatever limelight they can. Even if they're furious that Pride won, he is partially a Townsend Acres horse."

Samantha fumed to see Lavinia and Brad join Ashleigh and Mr. Townsend at Pride's head for the winner's photo. Afterward Samantha heard Lavinia mutter angrily to Brad, "They interfered with Lord Ainsley at the head of the stretch. I'm positive I saw Pride lug out."

"Le Blanc didn't say anything. He would have lodged a protest if there'd been any interference," Brad answered, surprisingly contradicting his wife. Samantha listened intently, but neither of them said any more, although Lavinia still looked furious. Then it was time to lead Pride to the backside.

"My thanks to you, Charlie," Mr. Townsend said before he left the winner's circle. "You and Ashleigh have done a wonderful job bringing him back. He certainly ran like a champion today."

"No thanks necessary," Charlie replied gruffly. But Samantha saw that Lavinia had overheard her father-in-law. Her expression was absolutely livid.

"What do you think?" Clay Townsend asked

43

Charlie and Ashleigh. "Should we point him toward the Suburban? Brad's entering Lord Ainsley. Or wait for Saratoga?"

Charlie rubbed his chin. "I think he'll be ready for the Suburban, but let's see how he comes out of the race."

"He looks pretty good to me," Mr. Townsend said with a smile.

"Yup. The race doesn't seem to have used him up."

"I'll stop by his stall later before I head back to Lexington," Mr. Townsend added.

Samantha had cooled, bathed, and fed Pride and had him back in his stall when Jilly returned from the jockeys' room after showering and changing. Craig was with her. Ashleigh and Charlie were outside Pride's stall discussing the race with a reporter from the *Daily Racing Form*.

"How'd he come out of the race?" Jilly asked when the reporter left.

"Fine," Charlie said. "Like he'd been out for an afternoon stroll. No signs of stress on his leg either."

"Well, Le Blanc wasn't very happy when I saw him in the jockeys' room," Jilly told them. "He said that after the race Lavinia and Brad ripped into him for the way he rode. Lavinia wanted him to lodge a protest, but he refused to because there wasn't any interference."

"I don't suppose Lavinia liked that," Ashleigh said.

"Nope, but believe it or not, Brad backed Le Blanc up and told Lavinia that lodging a protest against another jockey was serious and not something you did unless there was real evidence of deliberate interference."

"That just shows how little Lavinia knows about racing," Samantha said.

"Le Blanc told me that he did underestimate Pride—that he shouldn't have let him get away on the lead," Jilly added. "He said it won't happen again."

"Hmph," Charlie said. "Maybe we shouldn't race Pride in the Suburban. Causes too much trouble to have these two horses running against each other."

A moment later Mr. Townsend strode up to Pride's stall. "I'm on my way out," he said, "but I just wanted to check by and see how he's doing."

"No problems," Charlie said.

"It certainly was a worthwhile day for Townsend Acres," Mr. Townsend said happily. "Our horses running first and second. You'll be bringing Pride back tomorrow?"

"That's the plan," Charlie told him. "Give him a few days off. Then we can decide on his race schedule."

"I'll stop by Whitebrook, then," Mr. Townsend said. "Again, you've done a good job." He gave them a parting smile, then continued down the shed row toward Lord Ainsley's stall, where Ken Maddock joined him.

"Look who's here," Samantha said sourly. Brad and Lavinia were heading toward the barn with a group of their friends.

"Hope they stay out of our hair," Charlie muttered. As they passed Pride's stall Lavinia looked point-

45

edly at Ashleigh and Charlie, then spoke to her friends in a voice she knew would carry. "It's one thing to win a race fairly . . . but when you have to resort to sneaky tricks like changing race strategy at the last minute—well, it takes something away from the victory, doesn't it?" She smiled, and they drifted off down the shed row.

"If she doesn't keep her mouth shut, I'll shut it for her," Ashleigh growled.

"Don't waste your energy on her," Charlie said. "It's just talk."

"Talk that starts a lot of nasty rumors," Ashleigh answered, still fuming.

"What I don't understand," Jilly said with a frown, "is why Brad seems to be letting her run the show."

"I don't think he's letting her run the show," Ashleigh said dryly. "I think he agrees with everything she says and does, but it's easier to let her do the talking."

Jilly wagged her head. "They're a pair, aren't they? But at least you've got Mr. Townsend on your side."

"For now," Ashleigh said.

ALL SAMANTHA'S FRIENDS WERE THRILLED AT PRIDE'S VIC-
tory over Lord Ainsley. Maureen was only disappointed that with the school year nearly over, there
wouldn't be time for Samantha to write an article for
the paper. Tor had picked Samantha up at the airport,
and after congratulating her had told her happily that
he'd ridden Top Hat over the weekend for the first
time in over two months—and his arm hadn't bothered him at all!

"I have to go easy," he told her with a smile, "but I
should be able to ride Sierra this week for a light
work. I have to get myself in shape, too. We only
have four weeks until the Atlantic City steeplechase."

And they were going to be a full four weeks,
Samantha knew, with final exams and the junior
prom—and, of course, Pride and Sierra's continued
training.

There was other excitement at Whitebrook, too.

47

The Saturday after Pride's victory in the Nassau, his dam, Ashleigh's Wonder, arrived at Whitebrook with her three-week-old foal, a sturdy little colt. Ashleigh and Mike had vanned them over from Ashleigh's parents' Lexington farm, where Wonder had been staying for the past two years. Ashleigh was beaming as she led out the beautiful chestnut mare. Samantha guided Wonder's foal, although the tiny colt wasn't about to leave his mother's side and scrambled after her on long, gangly legs.

"I'm so glad you're here, girl!" Ashleigh said, kissing Wonder's nose. The mare nickered affectionately, then looked back to see if her foal was with her. When he safely reached her side, Wonder looked alertly at her new surroundings.

Clay Townsend was co-owner of the champion mare, who had been bred, trained, and raced at Townsend Acres, but when Townsend Acres had had serious problems with their breeding manager two years before, Mr. Townsend had allowed Ashleigh to take the mare to her parents' breeding farm. Now that Ashleigh was getting married, Mr. Townsend had agreed to let Ashleigh bring Wonder to Whitebrook. But there were conditions attached. He insisted that Wonder's foal of the previous year, Townsend Princess, go to Townsend Acres for her training.

"It broke my heart to see Princess vanned off to Townsend Acres," Ashleigh said, "even though it was Hank who picked her up. It makes me sick to think of Brad or Lavinia having anything to do with her training."

"I know what you mean," Samantha agreed.

"But at least Wonder is here," Mike said, trying to cheer Ashleigh. "And this little guy looks pretty special," he added.

Samantha rubbed her hand over the foal's brushy mane. "He looks like Pride, doesn't he?"

"His coat may end up a couple of shades darker," Ashleigh said, "but he looks good."

"Have you decided on a name for him yet?" Samantha asked.

"I was thinking about naming him Mr. Wonderful. Mr. Townsend seemed to like it."

Samantha chuckled. "Mr. Wonderful . . . yeah, I like it, too."

Charlie shuffled out of the barn toward them. Although he wasn't actually smiling, there was a happy twinkle in his eye as he greeted the mare he and Ashleigh had turned into a champion.

"Missed having you around, little lady," he said to Wonder as he laid a weathered hand on her sleek neck. "A fine little fella you've got there, too."

Wonder snorted her acknowledgment, then fondly nudged her nose against Charlie's shoulder.

"Haven't forgotten me, then?" the old trainer said, looking pleased despite himself. "They've been taking good care of you, I see."

"You bet we have, Charlie," Ashleigh said with a smile. "But now I think we ought to get them settled. You're going to like it here, girl," Ashleigh told Wonder. "And you can see your son, Pride, and your old friend Fleet Goddess. She's a mother, too, now."

They started across the stable yard to the mares' barn and the roomy box stall Ashleigh had prepared for Wonder's arrival. Once Wonder and the foal were settled, Samantha glanced at her watch. "I've got to go change," she said. "Yvonne's show is today. Tor's picking me up in a few minutes."

"Tell Yvonne good luck," Ashleigh said. "I hope she gets a blue."

"I think she just might," Samantha called as she hurried off to the cottage.

Her father was in the kitchen fixing himself a cup of coffee as she entered. He gave her a big smile. "I was watching through the window," he said. "It's good to see Wonder here. I guess Ashleigh's happy."

"She sure is. It helps make up for some of the aggravation Brad and Lavinia have been giving her."

Mr. McLean scowled. "It's always something with the Townsends, isn't it? Ashleigh deserves better." Ian McLean spoke from experience. He'd been an assistant trainer at Townsend Acres when he and Samantha had first moved to Lexington four years before. He'd had his share of run-ins with Brad and had left Townsend Acres for Whitebrook because of them. "You'd better get a move on," he added. "Tor should be here in a minute. And I've got to take a shower and get changed, too. I'm going into Lexington."

Samantha thought it strange that her father would be showering and changing to go into Lexington. He generally only went into town on errands, but she was in too much of a hurry to ask where he was going. She dashed up the stairs to her bedroom.

An hour later she and Tor entered the riding stable that Tor and his father co-owned. Samantha had driven part of the way into town, on some of the less busy roads. She had her driver's permit but had been so busy that spring that she hadn't gotten in enough practice to actually go for her driver's test.

Yvonne was inside the stable readying Cisco, the horse she would be riding in the advanced class. Earlier that spring Tor had brought Cisco over to Whitebrook to help with Sierra's training over the jumps. Yvonne had ridden him then and had liked him enough that she'd asked Tor if she could ride him regularly. Cisco had potential but needed some concentrated retraining that neither Tor nor his father had time to give. Yvonne had the time, and with Tor's guidance she'd really made progress with the gray Thoroughbred gelding. This was their first show together, though, and Yvonne was understandably nervous.

"Hi, guys," Yvonne called as Samantha and Tor walked up. "I'll be out in a minute. I'm almost finished with him." She tied off the last braid in the gelding's mane, stood back to inspect her work, and nodded. "I wasn't sure about the braids," Yvonne said, "but they came out all right."

"He looks great," Tor said, "and he knows it."

Yvonne nodded. "Now if he'll only stay clean until we jump." Yvonne was still in jeans, although she'd pulled her straight black hair back into a ponytail at the base of her neck. She came out of Cisco's stall and latched the door behind her. "Whew! Am I getting nervous or what?"

"Everybody's getting nervous," Samantha said.

"I don't know about that. There are a lot of people here from other stables, and some of them look pretty confident to me."

Tor laughed. "They're putting on a good face. I don't know too many serious riders who don't get a case of the jitters."

And Tor should know, Samantha thought. He and Top Hat had won their division at the National Horse Show in New York that past winter.

"So where's Gregg?" Samantha asked her friend. "I thought you said I was finally going to get to meet him."

"He's here," Yvonne said with a smile. "He took Maureen on a tour. They should be back in a minute."

"You're not competing against each other, are you?"

Yvonne shook her head. "If we were, I'd really be a wreck. He hasn't been jumping as long as I have. He's in intermediate."

"And doing really well," Tor told Samantha. "I'd better go," he added. "I've got to give my father a hand since we're hosting this show. I reserved some good seats for you guys. I'll join you as soon as I can." He gave Samantha's hand a squeeze before he hurried off in the direction of the stable office.

It was a beautiful, warm day, and most of the classes would be jumped in the big outdoor ring. Only the pony classes were going off in the indoor ring.

The stables, inside and out, were bustling. Horses were being groomed and walked. Tack was being polished. Riders and visitors walked up and down the aisles and gathered in clutches outside. The barn hummed with the sound of voices, most pitched low to avoid exciting the horses. The air was filled with the scent of leather, saddle soap, hay, and horse. Samantha loved it.

"Here they come," Yvonne said, uncharacteristically clasping her hands together nervously.

Samantha looked up the aisle and saw Maureen's familiar face. Walking beside her was a broad-shouldered young man. What made him stand out was his head of auburn curls. "A redhead like me," Samantha teased her friend.

Yvonne smiled.

"Hey, this place is great!" Maureen said enthusiastically. "Except the horses look so much bigger in person. And you guys actually ride them! Amazing!"

Samantha laughed. Maureen, at a stretch, was five feet tall. Samantha wasn't surprised the horses looked big to her. "You just have to get used to them, Maureen," she said. "After a while you don't even notice their size—unless you're at the wrong end of a kick or getting chucked out of the saddle."

"I think I'll stay on the ground and be a spectator," Maureen said.

Samantha had noticed Gregg and Yvonne exchanging a warm glance. Then Yvonne seemed to remember that Samantha and Gregg hadn't met. "Sammy," she said quickly, "this is Gregg Doherty. Gregg, this is my best friend, Samantha McLean."

Gregg smiled to Samantha. "I've heard a lot about

you from Yvonne. I've heard all about Pride and Sierra, too."

"You'll have to come out to Whitebrook sometime with Yvonne," Samantha responded with a smile.

"I'd like that. I want to get a firsthand look at a breeding farm. My parents inherited a lot of land from my great-grandparents and are talking about selling it. I'm trying to convince them to keep at least some of the land for pastures and raise horses. I've got a lot to learn, though."

"Cisco's set," Yvonne said. "Why don't you guys find your seats while I get changed?"

Outside, dozens of horses were being walked. Horse vans crammed the parking lot of the stable and spilled out over the lawn. Tor and his father should be happy, Samantha thought. Their show had drawn top competitors from all over the area.

They found their reserved seats, high in the central part of the nearly filled bleachers set up along the outside of the ring. Samantha saw Tor and his father talking to the judges, who were seated on a raised platform with a good view of the ring. Tor looked up, and she waved as they climbed to their seats. A few minutes later Yvonne joined them, looking elegant in her dress boots, tight-fitting beige pants, and crisp white shirt.

Within minutes the novice jumping classes began. Maureen, ever the reporter, had brought her camera and clicked away as young riders put their mounts over the dozen low but varied fences.

"Hey, Maureen," Samantha said teasingly, "save some film for Gregg and Yvonne."

"Oh, I've brought plenty. When do your classes start?" Maureen asked the two competitors.

Gregg checked his watch. "Mine should go off in about half an hour. In fact, I'd better get ready."

"Good luck!" they all called to him as he rose. Yvonne reached over and squeezed his hand.

"So what do you think?" Yvonne asked eagerly when Gregg was gone. "Nice, isn't he?"

"I thought so," Samantha said. Maureen nodded her agreement.

"He can be a little shy at first," said Yvonne, "but wait until you get to know him better. I thought I'd bring him over to Whitebrook one day this week to watch you work Sierra."

"Sure. Great idea. Maybe we can all take a ride afterward."

Forty minutes later Gregg entered the ring on a rangy bay, one of Tor's stable horses. None of the seven competitors before him had gone clean, although one had only two faults.

"You can do it," Yvonne whispered as Gregg put his mount into a canter and approached the first jump. Samantha and Maureen sat tensely, too, as Gregg started around the course. He and his mount went perfectly over the first nine fences, then there was a tight turn down the center of the course to a railed gate and a combination. Gregg misjudged the turn, taking it too tight. His mount clipped the rail with his rear hooves, knocking it down.

55

Yvonne groaned. "Four faults. He won't get the ribbon."

Gregg gamely collected his mount for the final two-fence combination, and they cleared that neatly. They exited the ring to a round of applause, but Samantha knew Gregg would be disappointed. They all went down to meet him as he rode off.

"Sorry," Samantha told him. "Except for that one rail, it was a beautiful round."

"Those are the breaks," Gregg said with a sheepish but disappointed smile. "But thanks. We still might get a second or third. I guess I'll keep him tacked."

They all stood with him as they watched the last two competitors jump. Unfortunately the last rider went clean, which meant Gregg was in third. "I guess I can't complain," he said more cheerfully. "It's only my second show. Next time we'll win it!"

"That's the way to think," Yvonne told him as Gregg remounted to go into the ring for the presentation. "My class is in less than an hour. After Gregg gets his ribbon, I think I'll go warm up Cisco."

"I'll go with you if you want," Samantha offered, knowing Yvonne might be less nervous having someone to talk to.

"Sure, if you don't mind. Maureen, you want to come, too?"

"I think I'll stay and watch the senior intermediate class. This is fun!"

"Okay, see you later."

Maureen headed back to the stands, and when Gregg rode out of the ring with the third-place ribbon fluttering on his mount's bridle, Samantha and Yvonne walked back to the stables. "This is the most nervous I've ever been!" Yvonne said. "Now I know how you must have felt before you rode Sierra in the steeplechase. Some of the riders I'll be competing against are really good! I mean, they've competed all over the place."

"You'll do fine," Samantha said. "Tor thinks you can win it, and he wouldn't say that if he didn't think it was true. But even if you don't, it's good experience for you."

"Yeah, I know," Yvonne agreed as they entered the stable building.

"I'll see you after I get my horse settled," Gregg called. "I'll meet you at the practice jumps."

Yvonne nodded, and she and Samantha went to Cisco's stall. Samantha helped Yvonne put the gelding in crossties and tack him up. Then Yvonne tied on her competitor number so it showed clearly across her back.

Behind the main stable buildings a small paddock had been set aside for warm-up, with a few basic jumps set up along one side. Samantha leaned against the rail as Yvonne mounted and entered the paddock and started trotting Cisco to limber him up.

A moment later Tor joined Samantha. "She getting nervous?" he asked.

"What do you think?"

Tor smiled. "She wouldn't be normal if she wasn't, but she'll do fine. The senior intermediate class is just finishing up. Then it'll take about fifteen minutes to set up the advanced course."

"What do you think of the course?" Samantha asked. "I know you had someone else design it."

"It'll be tough, but nothing Yvonne can't handle. The main problem she'll have is keeping Cisco together. You know how he loves to run between the fences."

Tor stayed with Samantha as Yvonne finished her warm-up. Gregg joined them as Yvonne rode out of the paddock.

"You did a good job today," Tor told him. "Except for misjudging that turn, it was perfect."

"Thanks!" Gregg said. "And I know my instructor would never lie."

Both he and Tor laughed. Tor walked over to Yvonne to give her some last-minute encouragement, then they all headed back to the ring. The riders in the junior advanced class were gathering near the entrance to the ring, ready to walk the course when the new fences were in place. Samantha saw a lot of tense and serious faces. Before Yvonne entered the ring with the other riders, Samantha gave her hand a squeeze. "Good luck! You're going to do great!"

"Boy, do I hope so!" Yvonne said tightly.

Gregg held Cisco, and Tor and Samantha headed to the bleachers to rejoin Maureen.

"Gosh," Maureen said as they sat down beside her. "Those fences are high! And look at that water jump. The horses can actually clear it?" she asked in amazement.

"They sure can, if ridden properly," Tor answered.

They were all silent as they watched the riders

walk from fence to fence. The course was much more difficult than the one Gregg had jumped, with tough combinations, tight turns, and twist backs. Samantha was glad she wasn't going out there to jump it.

Ten minutes later the riders had left the ring, and the first competitor prepared to ride in. "I'm glad Yvonne doesn't have to jump first," Samantha said. "At least she'll get a chance to see where the trouble spots are."

"Mmm," Tor agreed. "Five riders will go ahead of her, but there'll be six riders after her who'll have an even better opportunity."

"How many of these riders are in your classes?" Maureen asked Tor.

"Only three. And Yvonne's the best of those."

They lapsed into silence as the first competitor began. After the third fence she and her mount landed badly and fell apart, taking down two rails and landing inside the tape on the water jump. She looked miserable as she rode out of the ring. The next two riders didn't fare much better.

"This course is riding harder than I expected," Tor said, chewing his lip.

"You don't think Yvonne and Cisco can go clean?" Samantha asked.

"I didn't say that, but she's really going to have to keep him collected."

Two more competitors finished. The best round so far was six faults. Then it was Yvonne and Cisco's turn. Samantha clasped her hands together anxiously. "You can do it!" she whispered.

Yvonne's face was tight with determination as she saluted the judges, then circled Cisco in a collected canter toward the first jump, a gate. They sailed over. Yvonne looked ahead to the second fence, a parallel. They were over that, then the wall. Samantha could see that Yvonne had to keep a tight hold on Cisco as he tried to spurt toward the next fence. But she controlled him. They cleared a high brush, then went into the first of the tight turns toward a combination. Ahead was the water jump that had claimed many of the previous riders. Yvonne urged Cisco toward it, letting him lengthen his stride slightly so that he'd have the momentum to clear the wide obstacle.

He made a magnificent jump, his rear hooves touching down well beyond the tape. Samantha expelled a sigh of relief.

"Good," Tor said under his breath as Yvonne and Cisco successfully navigated a triple combination, a wide spread, another tight turn, a jump fashioned like a wishing well, and a double gate. Only three more jumps. Samantha crossed her fingers. Yvonne and Cisco had the best round so far. But there would be more competitors, Samantha reminded herself.

"All right," Tor murmured as Yvonne cleared the first of the last three fences. "Yes!" Then Yvonne and Cisco were heading to the last jump. "A clean round!" Tor cried as they landed. "Way to go, Yvonne! I almost don't believe it!"

"Wow!" Maureen cried. "That was amazing! I am *impressed*! Yvonne's better than I thought!"

The applause was loud and heartfelt as Yvonne

rode Cisco from the ring. Yvonne's beaming smile was ear to ear as she patted Cisco's neck.

"Shouldn't we go down and congratulate her?" Maureen asked.

"Wait until the other competitors have finished," Tor said. "There's always the chance there'll be a jump-off."

But to their delight, none of the remaining competitors jumped clean. Yvonne had won the blue ribbon!

6

AS PROMISED, YVONNE AND GREGG CAME TO WHITEBROOK one afternoon the following week to watch Sierra's workout. Since there were so many flat racers being worked in the mornings, Samantha and Tor frequently took Sierra out to the oval in the afternoons, when they had it to themselves. Tor was riding Sierra for the first time in months, and as Samantha, Yvonne, and Gregg watched, he took the colt through a clean circuit of jumps and came off the track grinning.

"Boy, does it feel good to be back in the saddle!" he cried. "Sierra's got his mind on business. If he keeps up like this, he'll definitely be ready for Atlantic City in three weeks."

"And with you riding, he'll have an even better chance," Samantha said. "What did you think?" she asked Gregg.

"Steeplechasing's a lot different from show jumping, but it looks like fun."

"It can be fun," Samantha said, glancing over to Sierra, who was tossing his head. "But you can have some pretty frustrating days, too, when Sierra's in one of his moods."

After they'd turned Sierra over to Len to be cooled out, they saddled up four of the exercise horses Mike kept on the farm and used in workouts to help pace or steady horses that were in serious training. When the horses were tacked, they set out for a ride over the grassy lanes and trails between and behind the green pastures of Whitebrook. Since the afternoon was warm, they didn't go too far, but Samantha could see that Gregg was really impressed with what he saw.

"Mike and his father put all this together themselves?" he asked Samantha.

"The basics were here," she answered, "but they had to make a lot of improvements, and Mike put in the training oval."

Gregg was frowning thoughtfully. "My parents' land was farmed once—most of the land is still cleared, but there's no fencing, and the barn needs work. It would be awfully expensive."

"When we get back from our ride, I'll introduce you to Mike," Samantha said. "He can tell you more."

Mike was in the stable yard when they returned. Samantha introduced Gregg, and Mike said he'd be glad to talk to him. As soon as the horses were untacked the two of them walked off, deep in conversation.

"I want to see Wonder and the new foal and Fleet Goddess and Precocious," Yvonne said excitedly after they'd put the exercise horses back in the paddock.

63

"You can see them all. Wonder's foal is adorable," Samantha told her. "Ashleigh wants to name him Mr. Wonderful."

"Neat name."

Len had already brought most of the mares and foals in for the afternoon, but Fleet Goddess and Precocious were still in the paddock. Samantha, Tor, and Yvonne watched the beautiful, nearly black mare and her two-month-old filly from the paddock fence.

"Precocious sure looks like her mom," Yvonne said admiringly of the tiny filly. "She's full of it, too, isn't she?"

Samantha smiled as she watched Precocious scamper over the grass on her long, knobby-kneed legs. Fleet Goddess looked on with tolerant affection as the little filly raced up and skidded to an awkward stop beside her.

"Wonder and Mr. Wonderful are already inside," Samantha said a few minutes later as she headed toward the rear door of the mares' barn. In the many immaculate stalls sleek mares were happily munching their evening meal with their foals nursing beside them. Wonder's stall was at the other end of the aisle. But as Samantha looked in that direction, she groaned.

"Oh, no, I don't believe it. What are *they* doing here?"

Brad and Lavinia were outside Wonder's stall, looking over the half-door.

"They must have come when we were cooling the horses. And Ashleigh's already gone home." Samantha strode forward. She didn't really want to confront them, but she wanted to know what they were up to. Over the weekend Ashleigh had gone to Townsend Acres to visit Townsend Princess. The yearling filly was in Hank's care and she looked fine, but Hank had told Ashleigh that Lavinia and Brad were already talking about "their" plans for the filly. Samantha didn't want them to start getting any ideas about the new foal.

Lavinia and Brad were so busy looking in at Wonder and the foal that they hadn't seen Samantha. She approached silently and heard Lavinia say to Brad, "I can't believe your father's seriously considering naming him Mr. Wonderful. I thought *I* was choosing the name for this colt. After all, he'll be coming to Townsend Acres when he's weaned."

"That's news to me," Samantha said as she walked up.

Lavinia and Brad started and turned around. Lavinia looked at Samantha as if she were some insect who had crawled out from the muck pile. "And what business is it of yours?" she asked coldly.

Samantha ignored the question. It really wasn't any of her business, but she wasn't going to let Lavinia get away with thinking she and Brad had any say about the foal's future. Samantha knew that Ashleigh and Mr. Townsend had made no decisions yet.

"Is there something I can help you with?" Samantha asked, making it clear from her tone that the two of them were not welcome in the barn. She was glad Tor and Yvonne were standing right behind her, lending her moral support.

"No, there's nothing *you* could help us with," Lavinia said. "I think we can look at the foal without any assistance."

Samantha felt like spitting in Lavinia's pretty face. She bit back the scathing comment she wanted to make. "I'm closing up the barn for the night," she told them.

"We were just leaving anyway," Brad said, unperturbed. He checked his Rolex. "We have to be at the Mitchells' in fifteen minutes, Lavinia. We'd better get moving." He took her arm and the two of them left the barn, but Samantha heard Lavinia's muttered comment: "I don't know *who* she thinks she is . . . this isn't the first time . . ."

Samantha glared after them.

"What a witch!" Yvonne murmured.

"I don't think Ashleigh's going to be very happy to find out they were over here," Tor said.

"No, she won't be," Samantha agreed. Ashleigh would be furious.

Yvonne and Gregg left twenty minutes later. Gregg was impressed with his conversation with Mike.

"Mike gave me a lot of tips about how to make repairs inexpensively—of course, I'd have to provide the muscle power," Gregg said with a smile. "He suggested that once the fences are mended, my parents and I could rent the grazing space out to make a little income."

"Sounds good," Yvonne told him.

Gregg nodded thoughtfully. "I'll have to sit down with my parents and make some plans, but I don't feel as overwhelmed as I did before I talked to him."

Gregg and Yvonne said good-bye and climbed into Gregg's car. Tor stayed a little longer, and he and Samantha checked in on Pride and Sierra one last time. Before leaving the barn, he gave Samantha a hug and a kiss. "I'll pick you up after school tomorrow. Do you still want to go into town for a movie tomorrow night?"

"Yes, I do."

"How about driving in after we finish up with Sierra and getting something to eat before the movie?" Tor suggested.

"Great!"

It was later than usual when Samantha went inside for dinner. She was still fuming about Lavinia and Brad's visit. She couldn't believe their nerve! She was deep in thought as she entered the kitchen. But as she glanced toward the stove, wondering if her father had started dinner, she stopped in her tracks. A strange woman was standing next to her father at the kitchen counter—an attractive woman with short, curly blond hair. Both of them seemed to be busily involved in preparing a meal.

"Sammy," her father said quickly, "I'd like you to meet Beth Raines. She stopped by to say hello, and I've asked her to stay for dinner with us." Even as he spoke, Samantha saw a tinge of what looked like guilt flicker across his face. "Ah . . . Beth and I have been seeing each other for a few weeks—"

Samantha's mouth must have fallen open, because Beth said with surprise, "Ian, you mean you haven't told her we've been dating?"

Mr. McLean flushed.

Beth came toward Samantha with a smile. "Well, I'm sorry I came as a shock to you, but I'm delighted to meet you. Your father talks so much about you." She extended her hand. Samantha numbly took it. Her father had started dating? And he hadn't told her? In the four years since her mother had died, her father hadn't seen any other women. The thought of him dating simply hadn't occurred to Samantha.

Samantha noticed that the table had been set, much more prettily than her father would have done. "We'll have dinner ready in a second," Beth said, still smiling, seemingly unaware of Samantha's reeling emotions. "Your father was making an omelet—his specialty, I know—but I thought I'd throw together a salad to make the meal a little more nutritious."

"Why don't you get washed up, Sammy?" her father said from across the room. He gave her a look that begged her to try to understand.

What is going on? Samantha wondered as she turned toward the bathroom. Normally Samantha would have washed up at the kitchen sink, but she needed some time to pull herself together. With no warning at all, she had walked into her own house to find a stranger taking over like she was already a fixture in their lives. When had Beth and her father started seeing each other? How could she not have known? She suddenly remembered him getting spruced up before going into town, and several nights he had gone out after dinner, but she'd been so busy with homework, she hadn't paid much

68

attention. He must have been seeing Beth!

When she returned to the kitchen, Beth and her father were putting the food on the table. They exchanged a quiet look and a smile. Samantha hadn't seen her father look at anyone like that since her mother had been alive. She felt a jolt of anger and dismay.

Samantha's mood didn't improve over dinner. Beth tried to be pleasant. She was smiling and friendly, but Samantha didn't miss the continuing looks her father and Beth exchanged—warm, private looks that Samantha instantly resented. Beth explained that she was an aerobics instructor at a health club in Lexington. Samantha wasn't wild about aerobics. If people needed exercise, why didn't they just get out and walk, or play tennis, or ride horses—anything other than jumping around like a bunch of netted fish. Beth also appeared to be an expert on nutrition and made several more remarks on diet during dinner. "You know, Ian," she said, "you and Samantha really should stay away from frozen dinners."

Samantha glowered. She prided herself on her cooking. It wasn't gourmet, but most nights there was a decent meal on the table, whether she or her father cooked it. "We don't eat many frozen dinners," she said.

Beth smiled. "But all these eggs aren't good for you either, you know."

Samantha looked over to her father, but he didn't seem the least upset. In fact, he seemed to be hanging on Beth's every word.

"So where did you meet my father?" Samantha asked coldly.

"Would you believe—in the grocery store," Beth said with a laugh. "Romantic, eh?"

Samantha scowled, upset that Beth should even mention romance.

"The bottom of my grocery bag broke," Beth continued, blissfully unaware of Samantha's reaction, "and your father helped me pick up the mess."

"That *was* a mess," Mr. McLean agreed. "Broken spaghetti sauce and juice jars all over the pavement." They laughed together over the shared memory.

"Oh, you don't make your own sauce?" Samantha quipped sarcastically, still stinging from Beth's comments about the McLeans' diet. "I mean, isn't the jarred stuff full of salt and additives?"

"Actually, usually I do make my own. I was buying the ready-made for my neighbor. Anyway, we stopped in town for coffee afterward," Beth continued, "and have been seeing each other ever since." They exchanged another look and silly smile. They reminded Samantha of a couple of lovesick teenagers. She and Tor never behaved so childishly. She wanted to throw up.

As soon as it was legitimately possible, Samantha excused herself from the table. "I have homework to do," she said. She didn't. She had already studied for her last final. "I'll come down and do the dishes when I'm done."

"Oh, don't worry about the dishes," Beth said with a smile. "Your father and I will do them. It was nice meeting you, Sammy. I'm sure I'll see you soon."

Samantha took her dishes to the sink, then hurried

upstairs. When the door was shut behind her, she sat down on the bed and dropped her head in her hands. She couldn't seem to control her churning emotions. She felt stunned, off balance, angry, and invaded. For four years, it had been just her father and herself, facing the good and the bad and coping together. Together they had dealt with their grief after Mrs. McLean's accident. Together they had tried to put their lives back on track. Samantha still missed her mother terribly. She'd thought her father did, too, yet here he was making a fool over himself with Beth, behaving as if Samantha's mother was long forgotten.

A half hour later Samantha reached for the phone on her nightstand and called Yvonne. Through her closed door, she could hear echoes of her father and Beth's happy conversation downstairs.

Yvonne listened silently as Samantha blurted out her distress, then said sympathetically, "I know it must have been a shock, Sammy. Your father should have told you that he was dating Beth instead of springing it on you like that. But you can't expect your father never to be interested in another woman. He must get lonely."

"The way he looks at her!" Samantha cried. "It's awful. It's like he's forgotten all about my mother."

"I'm sure he hasn't. And do you think your mother would want him to spend the rest of his life alone?"

"I don't know," Samantha said glumly. "I just don't like her. She acts like she knows my father as

71

well as I do—like they've got this private stuff going on—and I'm not part of it."

"Sammy, I think maybe you just got caught by surprise. She can't be all that bad. You won't feel so bummed about it tomorrow."

"Maybe not." But when Samantha hung up the phone, she wondered if Yvonne understood how she was feeling at all. Yvonne had never lost a parent. She couldn't know what it was like to have a stranger suddenly trying to take over the place of the mother she'd loved. Before she went to bed, Samantha picked up the photograph of her mother from the dresser. She felt her grief bubbling up all over again.

She climbed in bed and pulled the covers around her like a cocoon. A while later she heard a quiet knock on her bedroom door. She knew it was her father, but she felt too drained and confused to know what to say to him. She heard the door creak open and pretended she was asleep. A moment later it closed again, and there was the sound of footsteps retreating across the small upstairs hall as her father went to his room.

In the morning, as they were both rushing out for the daily regimen of workouts, her father briefly stopped her. "I'm sorry I didn't tell you about Beth, Sammy." He shrugged sheepishly. "I've been meaning to . . . but now you've met her. I know you're going to like her. She's a lovely woman."

Before Samantha could respond, he hurried out to the stables. Samantha stared after him, feeling a huge letdown. He hadn't said or done any of the things she wanted and needed. He hadn't hugged her or said he knew how upset she was—that her feelings were more important to him than Beth's.

Samantha did not have a good day. She didn't say anything more about Beth to Yvonne at school—just mulled over her distress silently.

Tor, at least, was more understanding when he picked her up after school, although in the end his advice was the same as Yvonne's. "It's hard, Sammy. My parents were divorced six years ago, and I still have trouble accepting my mother's second husband—as nice a guy as he is. But my mother's happy, and I think that's the important thing. Think of that."

Samantha tried to, and there were plenty of distractions to take her mind off her father's relationship with Beth.

As Samantha had expected, Ashleigh was furious when she told her about Lavinia and Brad's visit to Whitebrook the day before. "Where does she get the idea that *she's* going to name Wonder's foal?" Ashleigh stormed. "*She* doesn't have any interest in Wonder or her offspring! Mr. Townsend is the only one who does."

"She's married to his son," Charlie said tersely. "She and Brad figure that makes them co-owners, too."

"It doesn't!" Ashleigh cried, then she took a deep breath and tried to control her anger. "I know—I'm getting angrier than I should, but I absolutely lose it when Lavinia starts butting in. She's always trying to put me down—"

73

"She wants to run the show," Charlie said. "She's too used to her money buying everything she wants. This time it's not working. She buys Brad Lord Ainsley. He's a darned good horse, but Pride is better, and you train and ride Pride. You know more than she does about horse racing—you're showing her up."

"And you've done it the hard way," Samantha said. "Nobody gave you anything you didn't work for. That's really got to make her mad. Actually, I'd say she's jealous of what you've done."

Ashleigh sighed again. "It's silly to let her get me so upset. I've got enough going on!"

On Saturday afternoon the girls in Ashleigh's wedding party went into Lexington for the final fitting on their gowns. As the bridesmaids went into one dressing room, Ashleigh departed for another. "No one's seeing my dress until the day of the wedding," she told them with a teasing smile.

The bridesmaids tried on their dresses, and two seamstresses made final adjustments, tightening seams and shortening hems. Samantha loved the simply styled satin gown with its sweeping skirt. She'd never worn anything so glamorous.

"You look so grown-up in that dress," Jilly told her, "but then I forget that you're sixteen already. You couldn't have been much more than twelve when I met you."

"Right," Samantha said with a grin. "The track brat—that's what some of the kids called me in school. The wedding's going to be beautiful. Ashleigh was telling me how they're going to have tents all over the lawns and tons of flowers."

"It'll be nice all right," Ashleigh's older sister, Caroline, agreed. Caroline was maid of honor, and her dress was a slightly deeper shade of rose than the others'. It suited her fair good looks. "Let's just pray it doesn't rain."

"It wouldn't dare," Linda March, Ashleigh's longtime friend, said with a bright smile. "Not for Ashleigh and Mike's wedding!"

Linda glanced in the mirror, fluffed her blond curls, and turned from side to side to examine her dress. "It's kind of a shame they decided to put off their honeymoon until winter, though."

"I can understand," Jilly said. "They both have a really hectic schedule for the rest of the summer. It makes more sense for them to wait until it's quieter, when they can really relax."

"Ashleigh wants to go to the Caribbean," Caroline said. "I envy her! Justin and I will be scrimping after we get married this fall."

"But you've both got good jobs in Louisville," Linda said. "Pretty soon you'll be able to afford an exotic vacation."

When the seamstresses had finished, the bridesmaids all carefully removed their dresses and waited for Ashleigh, who appeared a moment later. She was all smiles, but she still wouldn't tell a thing about her gown. "You'll see it soon enough," was all she said.

It was late afternoon before Ashleigh dropped Samantha back at Whitebrook. Samantha hurried into the cottage to get ready for that night's junior prom. Tor would be picking her up at six thirty for the drive to the high school gym. She was really looking forward to the evening, and she bathed and dressed with a growing feeling of excitement.

The night turned out to be all that Samantha had expected. She had a ball. The band was great, and she and Tor were out on the floor for nearly every dance. Afterward she invited Yvonne and Gregg and Maureen and her date back to Whitebrook for a midnight snack.

They were all laughing as they entered the cottage. She heard the low rumble of the television in the living room. Her father had probably fallen asleep on the couch as he usually did. "There are chocolate-chip cookies on the counter and drinks in the refrigerator," she told the others. "Go on in. I'll just turn off the TV." The others went into the kitchen. Samantha stepped into the dimly lit living room on the left and headed for the TV. She'd wake her father and let him know she was home. Halfway across the room, she froze. Her father was asleep on the couch all right— but he wasn't alone. Beth Raines was curled up next to him with her head on his shoulder, asleep as well. Samantha felt the smile on her lips fade. The scene was so intimate! Stunned by what she'd seen, Samantha turned slowly and left the room for the kitchen.

The others were gathered around the kitchen table, smiling and talking quietly about the dance. Tor glanced over as Samantha entered the room and instantly frowned. He got up and came toward her. "What's wrong?" he asked softly. "You look like you've seen a ghost."

"Beth is here, asleep on the couch next to my father."

"They probably fell asleep watching TV," Tor said.

"He didn't tell me she was coming over."

"Maybe he just forgot to, Sammy. It's not a big deal. You shouldn't get so upset."

"I don't want her here," Samantha said stubbornly.

Tor gave her a level look and shook his head. "You're overreacting, Sammy. It's been such a good night. Don't ruin it for yourself. Come on, have something to eat," he added in a tone meant to cheer her.

Samantha followed him to the table. Fortunately the others didn't seem to notice her suddenly changed mood. She no longer had any appetite, even though she'd been starving when they'd arrived at the cottage. She nibbled on a cookie and listened with half an ear to what the others were saying. She couldn't put aside her feeling of betrayal—that her father was putting someone else in her place. After all, for four years it had been just the *two* of them. They had been happy. What right had this woman to break things up?

The others wanted to go out to the barn to see the horses. "Okay," Samantha said, "but we'll have to be quiet. We don't want to disturb them." Her thoughts were still on her father and Beth snuggled so cozily on the couch.

The stable cats followed them as they made the

rounds, walking quietly down the aisles, whispering their comments. Maureen especially was delighted with the tour, since she'd never been to Whitebrook before and had never had a close-up look at Wonder, Pride, and Sierra.

When the others had left, Tor put his arms around Samantha and gave her a kiss. "Cheer up, Sammy. It's been a wonderful night, and things will work out."

When she stepped back into the cottage, she went straight up to her room.

In the morning when she came downstairs, her father was sitting at the kitchen table.

"What's the matter?" he asked when he saw Samantha's expression. "Didn't you have a good time at the dance?"

"I had a fine time at the dance," Samantha answered coldly. "You didn't tell me Beth was coming over."

"I forgot—it didn't seem important." Her father scowled. "She came over to watch a movie, and we both fell asleep. Why are you acting like this, Sammy? Beth is a nice woman."

"I don't like her, and how can you do this to Mom's memory?"

"Samantha, I am not doing anything to your mother's memory. Not a day goes by that I don't think of her and miss her, but I get lonely. I need someone to fill the empty spaces in my life."

"You're not all alone! What about me?"

"You're everything to me, and you know it," her fa-

78

ther said quickly. "That will *never* change, but I need adult companionship, too—a woman's companionship."

Samantha didn't want to hear it. "I'm going to the stables," she said shortly, then rushed out the door into the morning air.

OVER THE NEXT FEW DAYS SAMANTHA KNEW SHE WAS
being distant and cool to her father, but she couldn't
help it. He talked to Beth on the phone every night
that he didn't go into Lexington to see her, and all too
often Samantha caught him staring off into space
with a foolish smile on his face. He didn't seem to
care what Samantha was thinking. She buried herself
in her work at Whitebrook, riding Pride and Sierra,
grooming them, and helping with Wonder and the
foal.

At school everyone was anticipating the last day of
classes. Tor and Samantha went to the junior-class
picnic at the Horse Park in Lexington and had a great
time playing volleyball and sharing their picnic lunch
with Yvonne and Gregg, Maureen, and some of their
other classmates. The picnic lasted until after dark,
when several juniors got out guitars and provided
the rest of the class with impromptu entertainment.

Samantha was sunburned and pleasantly exhausted when Tor brought her home, and she realized she hadn't thought of Beth and her father once all day.

Unfortunately she was in the stable yard when Beth drove down the drive the following afternoon. Beth waved cheerfully to Samantha, then breezed into the cottage without knocking. A few minutes later she and Samantha's father emerged, both smiling happily as he took Beth on a tour of the farm and introduced her to all the staff. Samantha was suddenly reminded of the hours her mother and father had spent in the stables, working happily together with the horses her father was training. Beth had admitted the first night Samantha had met her that she knew nothing about horses or racing. Samantha felt a crushing pain to see Beth at her father's side now, walking through the stables. To keep out of sight of them, Samantha went to the tack room and took out her frustrations on some dirty bridles.

There was already enough tension in the air at Whitebrook. Sierra would race in a week. Pride would race in the Suburban a week later against Lord Ainsley. Ashleigh and Mike were developing cases of prewedding jitters as they rushed around making all the necessary arrangements. Their wedding date was the Saturday after the Suburban.

To make matters worse, Lavinia and Brad showed up with Mr. Townsend late in the week as Samantha was preparing to take Pride out on the oval for a workout. Samantha saw Ashleigh clench her teeth in distress. Fortunately, Brad and Lavinia walked immediately to the rail of the oval and stood there talking to each other. Mr. Townsend came over to join Ashleigh and Charlie as Charlie finished giving Samantha instructions for the workout.

"How's he been going this week?" Mr. Townsend asked Charlie.

"I've got no complaints," Charlie answered. "I'm not asking too much of him. I just want to keep him fit and on his toes. Sammy's going to be slow galloping him today. No breezing." Charlie looked out toward the track, where two of Mike's horses were finishing their work. Mike was riding one, and his hired exercise rider the other. Ian McLean was at the rail, clocking the workouts. Samantha saw Mike glance in Lavinia and Brad's direction as he rode off the track and scowl. She knew from Ashleigh that Mike had had it with Lavinia and Brad. He would have told them to stay off his farm, only he was afraid doing that would create even more problems with the Townsends.

"Okay," Charlie told Samantha, "take him out. The track's clear."

Samantha started Pride forward toward the gap to the track. As she passed Mike he smiled to her and said in an undervoice, "Unwanted company again, I see."

Samantha grimaced, then urged Pride forward. She warmed him up at a trot and then a canter. Then, half standing in her stirrups, she let him out into a slow, collected gallop. She was glad the work didn't require much concentration or skill; Lavinia and Brad's presence unsettled her. But Pride could have done the work without a rider on his back. His strides were smooth and powerful. Samantha took him around the oval twice, then pulled him up, turned him, and trotted off the track.

As she passed Lavinia and Brad, she heard Lavinia say sneeringly, "They call *that* a workout? He looked like he was moving in slow motion. I guess the Nassau took too much out of him. We shouldn't have any worries about Lord beating him in the Suburban."

Samantha couldn't hear Brad's response. *You nit,* she thought of Lavinia. *That comment shows how little you know.* Charlie was pleased, though, when Samantha rode up. "Just right," he said, lifting his hat and wiping his brow with a red bandanna. He knelt to inspect Pride's legs.

"Will you be riding in the Suburban?" Mr. Townsend asked Ashleigh. As he spoke, Lavinia and Brad walked over. Neither of them seemed to notice that they weren't welcome. Samantha wanted to wipe the smug looks off their faces.

"I haven't made a decision," Ashleigh said to Mr. Townsend. Yet Samantha knew that Ashleigh had already asked Jilly to ride. She guessed that Ashleigh just didn't want to say so in front of Brad and Lavinia.

"Well, as long as we're here," Mr. Townsend said, "I'd like to take a look at Wonder's new colt."

"He's coming along great," Ashleigh told him as they walked off toward the paddock where Wonder was grazing and Mr. Wonderful was romping with the other young foals. Of course, Lavinia and Brad

83

followed, but not before they'd exchanged a look and a strange, almost secretive smile.

Samantha dismounted as Charlie held Pride's head. Charlie was shaking his own, and his lips were pursed. Samantha noticed that the old trainer's face was pale, but maybe that was because of the heat. "Is something wrong?" she asked with concern.

"Eh!" he answered disgustedly. "It's those two. Get on my nerves, and I don't like what it's doing to Ashleigh. Townsend told us while you were working Pride that he'll be away a good part of the summer. He's looking to buy into a breeding operation in England. That means you-know-who will be in charge."

"Oh, no." Samantha stared over to Lavinia and Brad, who were standing at the paddock rail watching Wonder and her foal.

"You got it," Charlie said.

So that's what their smug looks had been all about.

On a hot, sticky afternoon a week later, Samantha went into the barn to collect Sierra for a workout on the inner grass oval. It would be Sierra's last work before she, Tor, and Mike drove up to Atlantic City for Sierra's race. Tor had asked Samantha to ride because he wanted to study Sierra's movements and form, over the fences. Samantha knew Beth was at the farm because she'd seen Beth drive in and had seen her father and Beth head into the stable buildings. Samantha sure wasn't prepared, though, to hear their murmured voices as she passed an empty stall and to

84

look over and see Beth entwined in her father's arms, the two of them kissing.

Samantha nearly gasped aloud in shock, but neither of them had even noticed her. Red faced and shaking with an unexplainable emotion, she continued down the aisle, collected Sierra, and led him out the other side of the barn. She was too stunned and upset to say anything to Tor. She just got into Sierra's saddle and rode out to the track.

As Samantha warmed Sierra up she could already feel the sweat trickling down the back of her neck beneath her helmet from the afternoon sun. Just once around, Tor had told her. With the heat, neither of them wanted to work Sierra too hard, but this was an important work.

Samantha tried to concentrate, but all she could think of was the sight of her father and Beth in the barn. She felt the blood pound in her temples. What did her father see in the woman? What could Beth and her father possibly have in common?

At Tor's signal Samantha tried to shake free of her thoughts. She headed Sierra toward the first of the eight jumps, but the colt knew he had only half her attention. He raced toward the jump and hurtled over it. Samantha bounced in the saddle as they landed. She tried to put her mind to business as she collected herself, but Sierra had the upper hand now. They continued around the course, clearing all the jumps, but it was the sloppiest and most uneven performance they'd put in in ages.

Samantha knew what Tor's reaction was going to

be before she saw his face. She'd never seen him so upset.

"Sammy!" he shouted. "What were you doing out there? You let him walk all over you! That workout was absolutely worthless!"

Samantha cringed, but she knew Tor was right. The workout *had* been useless—even harmful because she'd let Sierra think he could get his own way.

"I'm sorry," she said as she dismounted. "I couldn't concentrate."

"Couldn't concentrate?" Tor said with disbelief. "He'll be racing in two days!"

"I can't help it. I'm upset about my father and Beth. She was here again today. I saw them in the stables, and—"

Tor didn't wait for her to finish. "Will you give your father a break? You're blowing the whole thing out of proportion!"

"No, I'm not!"

"Your father deserves to have some fun. He works hard enough. I don't think you're giving Beth a fair shake either."

Samantha felt angry tears sting her eyes. "You don't understand."

"Oh yes, I do," Tor shot back. "And I also know we have a big race coming up. Stop feeling sorry for yourself and think of that."

Samantha gaped at him. How could he talk to her like this? She felt an angry flush rising up her cheeks. By now she was too furious with him to tell him what she had seen that had so upset her. From the sound of it, he wouldn't care anyway.

Tor's expression softened a little. "Look, I'm sorry, Sammy. I didn't mean to yell, but we've worked so hard."

Samantha wasn't ready to forgive him so easily. Why couldn't he understand how *she* was feeling? And she knew perfectly well how hard they'd worked. She wasn't out to blow it, as he seemed to think.

"I'll cool him out," she said tightly. She walked off, leading Sierra. A moment later Tor joined her.

"Come on, Sammy," he said. "Don't be angry. We all say things we don't really mean."

Samantha's temper had the better of her. She wasn't giving in. "You meant it, though, didn't you?" she snapped angrily. "I'm just feeling sorry for my- self. All right! Have it your way!"

"But, Sammy, you *are* being—"

She cut Tor short. She knew what he was about to say. "I have things to do. What time are we leaving in the morning?" she asked coldly.

"Nine."

"Okay, I'll see you then." She stalked off, leading Sierra.

They were both tense the next morning as they climbed in the big horse van with Mike. Len was in the back with the horses. Mike had decided to bring a couple of his flat racers up to the Atlantic City track as well.

"Let's hope we bring home a couple of winners tomorrow," Mike said cheerfully. He seemed almost glad to get away from the farm and the steady stream of people coming by to talk to Ashleigh about preparations for their wedding ceremony and reception, which would both be held on the Whitebrook grounds. "I think our best hopes are with Sierra, though," Mike added. "The other horses I've brought aren't the best."

Samantha remained silent, remembering the horrible workout the day before.

"Sierra looked like he was on his toes when Len loaded him," Tor said. "This field will be a lot more experienced and competitive than the last, though."

"I know, but the way he finished in that last race after having so many problems early on gives me confidence," said Mike.

Samantha hoped Mike's confidence would be justified. As miffed as she still was with Tor, she could kick herself for allowing her concentration to slip so badly. Sierra was a horse who, given an inch, would take a mile. And she had sure given him an inch the day before.

Mike and Tor did most of the talking during the rest of the long journey. Samantha and Tor barely exchanged a word. He seemed to be angry now, too.

They were all tired when they finished settling the three horses in their stalls at the track. It was a much smaller track than anything Samantha was used to, and all the races were run in the evenings under bright lights. But it was a good place to build up Sierra's experience and confidence. The first three races on the card over the next two days were stee-plechases. The balance were flat races. Sierra was en-tered in the first race, a maiden allowance for three-year-olds and up at two-and-an-eighth miles. Since none of the horses had won before, they would get a break in the weight they had to carry. The purse was small, but if Sierra won, he'd start paying Mike back for the offer Mike had refused.

Len was staying at the stable dormitory. Mike had rented nearby motel rooms for the night—one for him and Tor, another for Samantha. They parted at the doors to their adjoining rooms.

"See you in the morning, Sammy," Mike said.

Tor seemed to hesitate, taking a step toward Samantha. Samantha stood tensely, not sure how to respond herself. Tor's face tightened and he gave her a brisk nod. "Night."

"Good night," she answered. Tor and Mike turned toward their room, and Samantha slowly turned to her door, wondering if she'd totally screwed things up. But she was so tired. All she could think of at the moment was a soft bed to fall on.

SAMANTHA OVERSLEPT THE NEXT MORNING. USUALLY SHE
woke automatically at five thirty, but when she lifted
her head from the pillow and looked at the traveling
clock she'd left on the motel room nightstand, she
saw that it was already seven.

She threw back the covers and swung her legs
over the side of the bed. She was surprised that Tor or
Mike hadn't knocked on the door to waken her.
Hurrying into the bathroom, she took a quick shower,
brushed her teeth and hair, and dressed in shorts,
sneakers, and a T-shirt.

A moment later she was out the door with her key
in hand. She knocked on the next door down. There
was no answer. Frowning in uncertainty, she walked
down toward the motel office, next to which was a
small restaurant. They wouldn't have left for the
track without her, would they?

As she looked through the plate-glass window at

the front of the restaurant, she saw them sitting at one of the tables. She quickly went inside.

Mike was facing the door and smiled when he saw her. "We were just going to call you. We slept late, too."

Samantha went over to the table and took the vacant chair between Tor and Mike. They both had juice in front of them, and Mike sipped from a cup of coffee. Samantha glanced over to Tor, feeling awkward. If anything, he seemed more distant than the day before. She knew her hotheaded temper had gotten her in trouble again. But then she remembered why she'd lost her temper, and that made her think of her father and Beth—and she felt something inside her tighten in pain.

"I didn't set my alarm," she said. "I usually wake up early."

"We were all tired from the trip," Mike said. "Len will see to the horses for us, and since they won't be racing until tonight, we might as well relax and have a good breakfast."

Samantha picked up the menu. But when she glanced again at Tor and saw his solemn expression, she lost most of her appetite. She hoped this wasn't how the rest of the day was going to go, because the hours were going to drag anyway, waiting for Sierra's 'chase.

The only conversation Tor made during breakfast was to discuss Sierra's schedule. "I want to take Sierra out and get him limbered," Tor said. "I gather the track will be open for workouts late this morning since there's no afternoon racing."

91

Mike nodded and took another sip of coffee. "I talked to the officials when we got in yesterday. Len's been here before, so he knows something of the setup and can point us around. It'll be a lot more laid back than Belmont," he added to Samantha.

"I figured that." But she knew she was still going to be a bundle of nerves.

They left the restaurant a half hour later for the track. There was far more activity on the backside than there had been the evening before, when the racing day was over and the horses had already been settled for the night. Len didn't seem upset that they were late arriving. He gave them all a grin and said he'd fed and watered their three horses and mucked out the stalls.

Sierra had his head over the half-door and was gazing about at his new surroundings as he chewed a mouthful of hay. As Samantha walked over to him, he pulled his lips back from his teeth. She laid her hand firmly over his muzzle. "Hey, cut it out, Sierra. I'm not in the mood for any fooling around today." Sierra's lips closed over his teeth again, and he eyed her as she lifted his lead shank off its hook and prepared to lead him out.

Tor was already collecting his working tack from the tack box outside the stall.

A few minutes later they led Sierra toward the track. Mike and Len followed with one of Mike's flat racers. Sierra pricked his ears and flared his nostrils as Tor rode him onto the oval. Samantha heard the colt snort excitedly, but he behaved himself as Tor jogged him twice around the oval. He came back barely blowing, and for the first time that day, Samantha saw a look of pleasure on Tor's face.

When they returned to the backside, Samantha bathed and groomed Sierra and helped Len out with the other horses—anything to keep busy. She didn't want to think about the race ahead, and she didn't want to think about Tor's continuing aloofness. By midafternoon they'd toured the grounds, had a late lunch in the track cafeteria, and had looked over the competitors in Sierra's steeplechase. And Tor had barely said two words to her. Several times he seemed about to, then changed his mind. It was getting to Samantha. Maybe she did owe him an apology, or at least a full explanation of why she had gotten so upset. Stubbornness and uncertainty stopped her. He hadn't wanted to listen and understand before. Why would he listen now?

When she took Sierra out for a walk and final grooming in early evening, she knew her mood was starting to affect the horse. She couldn't seem to think straight, and it was all Beth's fault. If she hadn't come into the picture, Samantha and Tor wouldn't have fought.

Sierra was getting skitterish, prancing and throwing up his head. Samantha had too little control of herself to calm the colt. She put him back in his stall and sat miserably on the bench outside. Tor had already collected his gear and headed off to the jockeys' changing rooms. Mike took Sierra to the receiving barn. The colt flared his nostrils and fidgeted as Mike led him off, and Mike cast Samantha a worried glance. Samantha sighed heavily, knowing Sierra's high-strung mood was at least partially her fault. She remained seated on the bench, feeling very much alone.

Len walked over and sat down next to her. "I can see you've got something on your mind. You that worried about Sierra's race?"

"Kind of," she admitted.

"Something else is bothering you, too." Len didn't say any more, but Samantha guessed that he'd noticed she and Tor had barely spoken to each other. For an instant, Samantha felt like blurting out to Len how confused and angry she felt, but she didn't.

In the end Len patted her knee. "Things will work out. He's a nice boy. You're a nice young lady."

Samantha shot him a look. So he *had* guessed. But Len was already rising and heading off to check on one of his charges. A few minutes later Samantha rose, too, gathered up her bag, and headed toward the saddling paddock.

She was waiting as Mike led Sierra in. The hour in the receiving barn didn't seem to have calmed Sierra down any. He looked around at the other horses in the ring, snorted, tossed his head, and tried to take a bite out of Mike as Mike tacked him up. Samantha held hard to Sierra's halter and pulled his head forward again.

"Let's hope he transfers some of this energy into a good performance," Mike said a little grimly. "Then again, he acted up before the other 'chase and you guys did okay in the end."

"Yes," Samantha murmured, "once he saw the field galloping away from him."

When Sierra's tack was in place, Samantha led him out around the lighted walking ring. She kept an iron grip on the lead shank as she noticed the colt's increasing excitement. She watched for the jockeys to arrive in the paddock.

A moment later they did. Most of them were amateurs, like Tor, but the majority of the riders had ridden in dozens of steeplechases. On average, the riders were bigger than flat-race jockeys since the allowable weights the horses would carry ranged from 138 pounds for maidens up to 155 pounds.

Tor was wearing Mike's blue-and-white colors. The same colors adorned Sierra's saddlecloth. Tor looked very professional as he crossed the ring toward her and Mike, but she noticed with a pang that his expression was still grim.

"He's pretty on edge," Mike said as Tor settled in the saddle.

"So I see," Tor replied, gathering the reins.

Samantha felt a lump growing in her throat. She wanted to say something encouraging to Tor, but she couldn't get the words out.

"Good luck!" Mike said before striding back to the box.

Samantha's stomach clenched as she started leading Sierra and Tor around the ring again. She had to say something. She couldn't stand the silence between them a second longer. "Tor . . ." she began.

Suddenly she felt the lead shank being dragged

through her fingers as Sierra reared up unexpectedly and slashed the air with his front hooves. Tor was caught by surprise. From the corner of her eye as she tried to get Sierra under control, Samantha saw Tor sliding over Sierra's rump to land on the ground.

Sierra came back down on all fours, and Samantha grabbed the side of his bridle, trying to keep him there. Mike rushed over to hold the other side of the bridle. Sierra rolled his eyes and snorted but stayed in place. Samantha looked back to see that Tor was already on his feet, but she knew the humiliation he must be feeling to have been dumped in the walking ring. She swallowed hard as he came around to remount.

"Tor," she said hoarsely. "I'm sorry. I know it's my mood that's upsetting him . . . and I shouldn't have been so angry with you . . ."

"We'll talk about it later," Tor told her, but she saw relief flicker over his features. He even gave her a quick, tight smile, then he turned all his attention to Sierra.

Mike walked with Samantha, holding the other side of Sierra's bridle as they finished the circuit around the ring. Then the horses were heading toward the course. Tor seemed to have Sierra under control, but Samantha's stomach was clenched in a knot as she and Mike went to the stands.

In the infield, the odds board flashed the final odds. After his performance in the walking ring, Sierra had gone from 10–1 to 20–1. The spectators sure didn't expect much from him. Samantha wasn't sure what to expect herself as she watched Sierra dance his way through the post parade. It was a fairly big field—twelve—and Sierra had drawn the number-six post position and would start right in the middle. Samantha wasn't happy about that either.

The horses were at the start. Samantha held her breath, then gasped with relief as Sierra broke sharply and went straight to the lead. He was a half-length in front as he and Tor approached the first fence. He leaped strongly over it and had gained a full length lead when he galloped away. Tor edged him in closer to the rail to save ground, but not too close. Samantha knew Tor wanted to leave himself plenty of maneuvering room. She was amazed that Sierra had gone so swiftly to the front—that the other horses and riders had allowed him to. She was also afraid that Sierra was so overexcited that he was running at the fences and lunging against the reins.

She studied Sierra's strides and Tor's grip on the reins. Tor had the colt on a tight hold. Sierra hadn't taken the bit in his teeth, and his strides seemed even enough, although she could see he wanted more rein than Tor was giving.

They cleared the second fence, the third, the fourth. Sierra maintained his length lead, but at times Samantha thought that he was jumping too boldly, trying to roar between the fences, challenging his rider. He and Tor had the advantage, with no horses ahead of them to avoid, but there was a lot happening behind them. Six horses jumped the third fence together. One went down; another stumbled, but recovered. Samantha saw Tor glance back under his

97

arm, then his eyes were instantly focused forward again at the next jump.

Sierra and Tor completed the first circuit, and still no horse had come up to challenge them. Through her binoculars, though, Samantha saw the signs that Sierra was getting bored. His ears pricked for an instant as he passed the grandstands. Maybe the noise had distracted him, but she thought otherwise. She'd ridden him in too many workouts and knew that pricked ears meant he'd suddenly lost interest. Tor woke him up by twitching the reins. Sierra's ears flicked back, but he'd slacked off on his stride, and one of the other horses closed rapidly as they approached the next fence. He was a head behind Sierra as they hit the takeoff point. Sierra must have seen the other horse, because he thrust powerfully with his hindquarters and landed far out from the fence, regaining his lead, but not by much.

They continued down the backstretch through the second circuit, Sierra and the horse beside him fighting for the lead. But as they approached the final turn and the last fences, the late closers were starting to make their bids. It seemed to Samantha that a wall of horses was suddenly making incredible progress, closing the gap between themselves and the leaders. Samantha had been afraid all along that Sierra wouldn't have enough left to beat off late challenges. She was doubly frightened now.

Sierra and Tor came off the turn with a half-length lead. They had one more fence and the run to the wire. She saw Tor glance under his arm again. He saw the others coming. She felt as if she was in Sierra's saddle with him. What would *she* do? Give Sierra full rein and knead her fingers hard on his neck to encourage him to put out his full effort now . . . or have patience and wait? But if Tor waited, it might be too late.

From what Samantha could see, Tor didn't have to make the decision. He and Sierra landed off the last fence with three horses beside them. Sierra, seeing the horses challenging him, took off like a cannon shot for the finish line. Tor gave him all the rein he wanted. To Samantha's delight, the big colt sprinted off toward the finish like a fresh horse.

"Go!" Samantha screamed as Sierra continued to power forward. Samantha was sitting so close to the end of her seat, she nearly slid off. Sierra increased his lead from a nose off the last fence to a length and a half by midstretch. When he and Tor streaked under the wire, he had a two-length lead. They'd won it! She jumped up at the same moment that Mike did.

Mike was grinning broadly. "After the way he was behaving before the race," he said, "I honestly didn't think he could win. How the heck did Tor get him to settle?"

"Tor's a good rider," Samantha said, "but I think Sierra had something to do with it, too. He can't stand to have a horse in front of him."

The presentation to the winner was modest, but the happy grin on Tor's face was all the reward Samantha needed, especially when he leaned down out of the saddle to her and said, "Let's go someplace alone tonight, have a pizza, talk . . ."

"Yes," she said.

Sierra's performance had definitely surprised a few people and sparked interest. As they cooled and settled him, a steady stream of people stopped by to have a better look at the colt. Samantha was thrilled by the attention Sierra was getting, but she couldn't wait to go off with Tor and sort out things between them.

At last, they walked to a nearby restaurant and found a quiet corner table where they could talk over their pizza. Samantha babbled out her regrets about her temper, finally telling Tor why she had been so upset that she'd ruined Sierra's final workout. "When I went to get Sierra, I saw my father and Beth in one of the stalls . . ." Samantha swallowed and felt a rush of blood in her cheeks just remembering their intimate embrace. "They didn't even know I was there. I was so shocked to see them kissing like that . . . and embarrassed and angry . . . and, I don't know . . . I felt like I'd been kicked or something." Samantha shook her head. "When I took Sierra out on the oval, I couldn't get it out of my mind. I knew I'd messed up the workout, but then when you started yelling at me, I totally lost it."

Tor reached over and took her hand. "I'm sorry, Sammy. I just wish I'd known the whole story. Now I can see why you were so upset. You had reason to be."

"You didn't seem to want to listen."

"I know. I didn't listen. All I could think of was that Sierra was racing in a day and you were more interested in your father's relationship. I jumped to conclusions, and I don't blame you for being angry. Of course, I didn't understand then *why* you were so mad at me," Tor added. "When you barely said two words during the whole trip here, that made *me* angry. I thought you were still feeling sorry for yourself."

"Your yelling at me was just too much on top of what I was already feeling," Samantha said softly. "But I shouldn't have lost my temper with you."

"I can see now why you did. Look, Sammy, I know it's been hard for you losing your mother, and you're having trouble accepting Beth. Maybe you should talk to your father about how you're feeling." Tor paused and squeezed her hand.

"Maybe."

"We both made mistakes yesterday, but is it okay now?" Tor gave her a questioning look with his blue eyes. "Have we sorted everything out?"

Samantha looked at him, then smiled with huge relief. "Yes," she said. "I think we have. And let's never have another argument. I hate it!"

Tor smiled, too. "So do I."

Samantha realized more than ever how special their relationship was. And Tor was right. Maybe she should talk to her father about her feelings, but he seemed so wrapped up in Beth, she wondered if he'd see Samantha's side at all.

Later, they walked back to the motel arm in arm under a starlit sky. It was a beautiful night, and Samantha felt as if a load had been taken off her shoulders.

9

THEIR RETURN TRIP TO WHITEBROOK THE NEXT DAY WAS A happy one. Samantha and Tor were back on good terms. Mike was thrilled with Sierra's win, and two of the horses he'd brought had been ridden to victory by a local jockey. It had been a very successful day for the farm.

The next days were busy, too, as Samantha, Ashleigh, and Charlie readied Pride for the Suburban at Belmont that weekend. Samantha didn't have time to think about her father and Beth, or to talk to her father about her feelings. She pushed it all to the back of her mind.

Charlie would fly up to New York with Pride. Ashleigh, Mike, and Samantha would travel on a regular passenger flight. Samantha carefully packed what she would need for the six-day trip and helped Charlie clean and sort all Pride's gear. Pride was in top shape and breezed impressively through his final workout. Samantha and Ashleigh felt confident as they left for the airport early Tuesday morning.

On their arrival at Belmont, though, none of them felt as cheerful. Lord Ainsley was already there in the Townsend Acres stabling, together with a half-dozen other Townsend Acres horses. They discovered that the end box stall that Pride usually occupied had been assigned to another horse. Pride had been given a stall right in the middle of the row, where he would be guaranteed the least amount of peace. Pride's end stall was now occupied by one of Townsend Acres second-rate horses, who raced in the bottom claiming ranks. Lord Ainsley had been given the big box stall at the opposite end of the row.

Ashleigh was livid. None of them had any doubts about who had rearranged the stabling.

"I'll get them to change it," Ashleigh said. "This is ridiculous!"

"Don't waste your breath talking to the Townsend kid and his wife," Charlie told her. He was scowling and his jaw was tight. "I already talked to Maddock and Hank. Maddock couldn't believe what they'd done either. We'll change the stabling around in the morning, whether the younger Townsends like it or not."

Of course, Lavinia did not like it at all. She arrived on the backside early the next morning after the switch had been made. Samantha was tacking up Pride in the stall so Ashleigh could take him out for a light work.

"What's going on here?" Lavinia demanded. "That's not the stall he was assigned to."

"This is the stall he normally has," Ashleigh answered coldly. "I'm not stabling him in the middle of the row where the noise and commotion can bother him."

"Brad and I will decide what horses go where. We're paying for the stabling. Move him back where he was assigned."

"He's not going anywhere," Charlie said. "We're not moving Pride so that you can put a second-rate claimer in the best stall."

Ken Maddock had heard the raised voices and left the horse he was saddling to walk over. "I agreed to the switch," he told Lavinia. "Matchlight will be lucky if he places. He doesn't need any special treatment—it wouldn't make any difference to his performance. Pride is an altogether different story."

Lavinia stared at Townsend Acres' head trainer. Samantha could see the frustrated fury on her pretty face. Lavinia must have known that in this case she couldn't order Ken Maddock around or make vicious threats. Clay Townsend would never back her up. He had the final say, and he wanted only the best for Pride.

"We'll see about that!" Lavinia said huffily, then she spun on her heel and stormed off.

"Thanks," Ashleigh said to Ken Maddock.

Maddock was staring after Lavinia, shaking his head. "No thanks necessary. I've only agreed to the sensible thing, and frankly, I'm getting a little tired of her trying to throw her weight around. I wish Townsend Senior was more observant. Then again, she's sweet as pie to his face."

"Well, we've got horses to work," Charlie said. He looked down the row to where Hank was leading Lord Ainsley out of his stall. "You working him this morning?" he asked Maddock.

"Brad's riding him. He decided he wants to give Lord his last work before the race." Maddock scowled and walked off to join Hank.

"He doesn't look very happy about it," Samantha said.

"He's probably afraid Brad will work Lord Ainsley too hard," Ashleigh replied. "Brad isn't known to listen to a trainer's instructions."

"Well, if he works him too hard, it's to our advantage," Charlie said. "Let's go."

Samantha stood beside Charlie at the rail as Ashleigh rode Pride out onto the oval. A moment later Mike joined them. "I hear I missed some fireworks," he said.

"Yup, but it worked out all right." Charlie squinted his blue eyes in the direction of Ashleigh and Pride. Samantha noticed the old man's face looked haggard, but after the run-in with Lavinia, she wasn't surprised.

As Ashleigh warmed up Pride and moved toward the first turn, Brad urged Lord Ainsley onto the oval. The big bay looked sharp, Samantha thought. He was obviously in top form for the race. But so was Pride, she reminded herself. Ashleigh kept Pride to a jog as they came down the backstretch. She and Charlie had agreed that Pride needed only a light gallop to keep him on his toes.

At the top of the stretch Ashleigh let Pride out a notch. There were several other horses working, but they were spaced well apart on the big track. During workouts riders tended to stay clear of other riders and horses, unless a pace horse was being used.

Pride continued smoothly at a slow gallop, with Ashleigh half standing in the stirrups. Samantha saw that Brad had let Lord Ainsley out into a gallop, too, but a less constrained one. They were closing the distance between them and Ashleigh and Pride. Ashleigh had Pride in fairly close to the rail. There was the whole width of the track outside of them if another rider wanted to pass. Brad was bringing Lord Ainsley up alongside two paths out, but instead of galloping past Ashleigh and Pride, he held Lord Ainsley just off their flank, slowing his pace to match Ashleigh and Pride's.

"What the heck does he think he's doing?" Mike cried.

"I know what he's doing," Charlie muttered, "but I can't believe he's got the gall to try it."

"He's trying to pressure Pride, isn't he?" Samantha asked. They all knew that if Pride saw a horse coming up alongside of him, he would automatically fight to increase his pace. Brad knew it, too.

Sure enough, Pride had spotted Lord Ainsley. Samantha could see that Ashleigh was struggling to hold him. Pride was trying to lunge forward against her hold. Despite the pressure on his reins, he increased his speed. Samantha gasped when she saw Brad increase Lord Ainsley's speed, too—just enough to move up even with Pride. Pride reacted, trying to increase his speed again. Ashleigh was doing all she could just to hold him. He plunged against her hold as the two horses came galloping down the stretch.

"I'll break that kid's neck!" Charlie growled. "Pride's going to come off the track undone." Charlie was about to stomp over to Ken Maddock, whose expression was grim as well, when Brad suddenly gave Lord Ainsley rein, and they shot past Pride and Ashleigh and roared on up the track.

Ashleigh was still struggling to hold Pride, who seemed intent on going after them. Finally Pride's good manners won out.

He stopped fighting Ashleigh, although he tossed his head in frustration. Samantha saw that his coat was soaking with sweat. Ashleigh let him gallop out his frustration for another quarter mile, then she slowed him to a jog, circled him to the outer rail of the track, and trotted back to the gap.

"I'm lodging a complaint with the stewards," Ashleigh said through gritted teeth. "He could tell we were out for a light gallop. He was deliberately pressuring Pride! I was screaming at him out there to go on by. He wouldn't even look at me. He and the witch probably planned this to get Pride as unsettled as possible."

Pride was still showing the effects of the experience. He huffed and danced his hindquarters around as Ashleigh tried to dismount. Mike gave Samantha a hand holding the horse, who normally behaved with gentlemanly calm after a work. Charlie was already running his eyes over the excited animal. He waited till Ashleigh was on the ground, then quickly removed Pride's saddle. "Let's get him to the backside and cooled out," he said.

As she prepared to lead Pride away from the oval, Samantha glanced over and saw Brad and Lord Ainsley ride off the track. A few sharp words passed between Brad and Ken Maddock. Ashleigh was already storming off in Brad's direction. Brad turned from Maddock and met her halfway.

"What do you think you were *doing* out there!" Ashleigh cried.

Brad raised his hands in a defensive gesture. "Look, sorry," he said. "I couldn't get him to move past you."

"Like heck!" Ashleigh told him.

Brad's expression was a picture of surprised innocence. "Honestly," he said. "He dropped right off the bit. There was nothing I could do to keep him going. Then suddenly he kicked in again. I couldn't be sorrier if it upset Pride."

Sure, Samantha thought, but she knew that if Brad was going to give that explanation, there was no way Ashleigh could prove he'd deliberately pressured Pride.

"I don't buy it, Brad," Ashleigh said, "but unfortunately I can't prove otherwise. Just stay away from Pride." Ashleigh spun on her heel. Her mouth was still tight with anger. Samantha saw Lavinia, who was standing behind Ken Maddock, smile with mocking satisfaction. That smile convinced Samantha that Brad's ride had been no accident.

She told Ashleigh as much as they walked Pride to the backside. "Oh, I know he was lying through his teeth," Ashleigh said. "But I really can't prove anything. We'll just have to be constantly on our toes, waiting for their next trick. What a waste of time and energy!"

Samantha immediately went to work on Pride, bathing him, walking him, grooming him, pampering him, until the excited horse calmed down. She felt drained when she finally left his stall. Two and a half more days until the Suburban. How were they going to get through it? She prayed Mr. Townsend would make an appearance soon and not wait until the afternoon of the race.

They all kept a close watch on Pride. Hank was on the alert, too, but the rest of the afternoon and evening passed without a problem. Neither Lavinia nor Brad came to the backside.

The next morning Samantha and Ashleigh arrived at Pride's stall to find Ken Maddock talking to Charlie. Maddock looked upset and sullen.

"Sorry about what happened yesterday," Maddock said to Ashleigh. "I feel bad about it. Brad still claims that Lord dropped the bit. It doesn't wash with me, but I'm not in a position to contradict him. The Townsends pay my wages. Anyway, there's other news. Lord came up lame this morning."

"I'm sorry," Ashleigh said sincerely. "What's wrong?"

"Not sure. He didn't show any sign of a problem

109

when we cooled him out yesterday. He may have kicked his stall during the night . . . I don't know. I'm having the vet look him over."

Samantha thought it was just as likely that Brad had worked Lord Ainsley too hard the previous morning. "Does that mean he won't race Saturday?" she asked.

"I don't know," Maddock answered. "I'll see what the vet has to say, but I'm certainly not going to run him if there's even a question of a problem."

"Wouldn't be worth the risk," Charlie said. "But it's too bad after all the work you put in to have to scratch him at the last minute."

"It all goes with this business, doesn't it?" Maddock straightened. "I'll let you know how it goes. Townsend Senior is due in tonight, by the way."

Good! Samantha thought. Mr. Townsend would keep Brad and Lavinia in line. The fact that Lord Ainsley might not even run didn't comfort Samantha. Who knew how Lavinia and Brad would react to the news?

After Samantha had walked and groomed Pride, she went to one of the pay phones on the backside and put in a credit-card call to Tor at the stable. Thankfully she got him when he had a few minutes free. She told him everything that had been going on. She could imagine him shaking his head in disgust at the other end of the line. "I just don't believe them," he said.

"I think it's more than Lord Ainsley beating Pride," Samantha told him worriedly. "They want their horse to win, but they want to get to Ashleigh, too. They don't want her to have any control. You know how much they both hate Ashleigh's success."

"But they never actually step far enough over the line so you could nail them. Hang in there," Tor said. "I miss you."

"Miss you, too," Samantha said wistfully.

"I'll be watching the race on Saturday. Call me afterward as soon as you get a chance."

"I will," Samantha promised.

Later that afternoon Ken Maddock told them that Lord Ainsley definitely wouldn't be running. The vet had found no serious injury, but there was swelling in his left rear ankle, maybe the result of a bruise. They were icing it, but there was no way that Maddock was going to risk running him Saturday.

Samantha had mixed reactions to the news. On the one hand, she was relieved that some of the pressure would be off Pride. On the other, she wondered what new obstacles Lavinia and Brad might try to throw in his path.

An hour later Samantha heard raised voices at the other end of the shed row. She was in Pride's stall checking his water and hay, and she remained hidden there as she listened.

Lavinia's angry tones carried clearly. "What do you mean you're pulling him out of the race? It's only a bruise, and he'll have two days to mend."

"It's not enough time." Maddock sounded irritable and at the end of his patience.

"Of course it is," Lavinia said haughtily. "Brad and I want him in this race. We *are* the owners. We have final say."

"If you want this to maybe be his *last* race," Maddock shot back, "then go ahead and run him. But you won't find me in the saddling paddock. I won't have any part of it."

Samantha chanced a glance around the edge of the stall. Neither Lavinia nor Maddock was looking in her direction. She saw Brad walk up. He'd obviously heard Maddock's last comment. He was frowning, but his words surprised Samantha. "Maddock is right," he said to Lavinia. "We can't risk running him. I'm as disappointed as you are—I'm sick and tired of Ashleigh Griffen having it go her way all the time—but there'll be other races. They won't beat us next time out." There was something in his tone that sent a chill down Samantha's spine. What were they up to now?

Mr. Townsend arrived that night, and during the next two days there was relative calm at the Townsend Acres stabling, but Charlie and Ashleigh both looked as if they were waiting for the next bomb to fall. By Saturday afternoon, as Samantha and Charlie led Pride into the saddling paddock, it hadn't fallen yet. Pride was in good shape. Ashleigh had jogged him on the track the previous morning, and he'd gone smoothly. With Lord Ainsley out of the race, Samantha felt confident that Pride could win it easily. The rest of the field weren't of his caliber, but she fought against overconfidence. Anything could happen in a horse race.

Mr. Townsend was standing with Ashleigh and Mike in the saddling box. Samantha wondered how much he'd been told of his son and daughter-in-law's behavior earlier in the week. There was no sign of Brad or Lavinia—thank heavens. Jilly had arrived that morning, fresh and eager to ride, but she admitted to being relieved, too, that Lord Ainsley had been scratched. Jilly knew that if Lord Ainsley had raced, Le Blanc wouldn't have given her and Pride an easy time of it.

There was still no sign of Lavinia and Brad by the time the horses were saddled and the jockeys had entered the ring to mount and go out to the track. As Samantha led Pride and Jilly through the final circuit of the walking ring, the crowd cheered Pride. They had every confidence in him.

Their confidence was well-founded. Pride dominated the race from start to finish. Samantha shouted her excited encouragement as Pride led the field down the backstretch by an ever-increasing margin. At the end of the far turn, he changed leads and accelerated with a new burst of speed. The crowd was on their feet, roaring in excitement as Pride's lead increased to fifteen lengths. The rest of the field looked as if they were standing still. By the time Pride and Jilly flashed under the wire, Pride was clear by sixteen lengths, and he'd done it effortlessly! He barely seemed winded. The cheering in the grandstands was deafening. The fans had their star, and it was Pride.

Calls of congratulation came from all sides as Samantha, Ashleigh, Mike, and Charlie made their way to the winner's circle. Mr. Townsend was already there, looking incredibly pleased. But now Lavinia and Brad were with him. Samantha noticed Lavinia giving Ashleigh a look of such absolute dislike that Samantha momentarily shuddered. But fortunately Ashleigh hadn't noticed, and Samantha tried to put it out of her mind, too, as she took Pride's head and kissed him soundly on the nose.

"You were incredible!" she murmured, still feeling a little awed by his performance. Pride huffed an excited breath as Jilly dismounted and removed the saddle to weigh in.

By the time Jilly returned to remount for the winner's photo, Lavinia and Brad had followed Mr. Townsend to Pride's side. Samantha wasn't surprised that they wanted to be in the photo, even if they were having a very difficult time looking pleased. What surprised her was the venom in Lavinia's voice as she muttered to Brad, "This won't happen again."

10

SAMANTHA GAVE ASHLEIGH ALL THE HELP SHE COULD IN the five days leading up to Ashleigh and Mike's wedding. Pride's smashing victory had lifted spirits, but Ashleigh and Mike were both frazzled making last-minute preparations. A crew of workmen came to set up striped tents on the lawns for the reception buffet. The girls in the wedding party all went into Lexington to collect their dresses. Mike, Mr. Reese, Mr. Griffen, and Ashleigh's younger brother, Rory, went into town, too, to be fitted for their tuxedos. Ashleigh went through checklists and final details with the caterers and the florist. Her mother frequently came over to help her.

The only sore spot for Samantha was that Beth was at the cottage so frequently in the evenings. Without asking Samantha she took over dinner preparations, and later sat on the couch with Mr. McLean, watching television or reading and listening to music. On

115

Wednesday, Tor came to pick Samantha up to go to the movies. Samantha's father had gone to the barn to make a last check of the horses. Beth was in the kitchen and waved Samantha off. "Have a good time. Don't be too late."

Samantha nearly lost it. Who was Beth to tell her when to get home? She was fuming as she went out to meet Tor and had to take several deep breaths in order to calm down. She wasn't about to bring up the subject of Beth to Tor, but Beth had succeeded in getting another black mark in Samantha's book.

The following afternoon Yvonne and Gregg came over to take a trail ride with Samantha and Tor. They were just getting ready to collect the horses from the paddock when Samantha saw Brad's Ferrari coming down the Whitebrook drive. Brad parked under the trees at the side of the drive, and he and Lavinia got out. Samantha could barely believe her eyes—how could they have the nerve to show up at Whitebrook after all the trouble they'd caused in New York?

Ashleigh and Charlie were talking outside the stable office. Samantha saw them turn and gape, too. Brad and Lavinia walked across the yard as if they owned the place. They stopped at the paddock where Wonder and her foal were grazing without even acknowledging Ashleigh. Ashleigh, her lips tight with anger, strode after them. Unfortunately Mike was in town running errands, but Samantha wasn't going to leave Ashleigh to deal with the Townsends alone. She followed the older girl. Tor walked with her. Charlie shuffled over, too. His blue eyes were shining and he was muttering angrily under his breath.

Ashleigh had reached Lavinia and Brad. "What are you doing here?" she asked icily.

Brad and Lavinia turned from the paddock rail. "Checking on the foal's progress," Brad said lazily. "Since my father's in England, we want to make sure everything's coming along smoothly."

"You're not welcome here," Ashleigh said with steel in her voice. "Please leave."

Brad raised his brows, then smiled. "Oh, I think we have every right to inspect our property."

"Wonder and Mr. Wonderful are not *your* property. You're trespassing."

"I'm afraid you're way off base, Ashleigh," Brad said with a sneer. "In my father's absence, we're acting on his behalf."

Lavinia casually tossed her shining blond hair behind her ear. "Oh, by the way, we're changing the foal's name. Mr. Wonderful is so pedestrian. We've decided to call him Lavinius when his papers are filed."

Samantha's gasp was audible.

Ashleigh glared at Lavinia. "You can't do that."

Lavinia smiled with satisfaction. Then the Townsends turned and headed back to the Ferrari. Ashleigh looked ready to storm after them, but Charlie laid a restraining hand on her arm and wagged his head.

"Let it go," he said. "You won't get anywhere with them. Call Clay Townsend. Maddock will have a number where to reach him in England."

117

Ashleigh's face was absolutely white. Samantha would gladly have strangled Lavinia for what she was doing to Ashleigh. "Lavinius." Samantha practically spat out the word. "Who does she think she is— naming Wonder's foal after herself?"

"Before we get carried away," Charlie said gruffly, "let's call Townsend. Can't believe he knows what's going on."

Ashleigh and Charlie strode off to the house, and the others turned to each other.

Yvonne looked dazed. "They think they can get away with absolutely anything. It's unreal."

Ashleigh's conversation with Mr. Townsend didn't totally resolve things either. He told her that he had signed some Jockey Club registration forms before he'd left, but they had been early registration forms for several foals at Townsend Acres. He, Brad, and Lavinia had discussed naming one of that year's Townsend Acres foals Lavinius, but Mr. Townsend hadn't been thinking of Wonder's foal. Brad and Lavinia must have misunderstood. In any case, he'd be flying back to the States the following day and would straighten it out. Ashleigh said that during their call, Mr. Townsend had sounded as if he had more important things on his mind than the naming of a foal.

Nerves were stretched tight at Whitebrook on Friday. Charlie was an absolute grouch, barking at everyone. Even Mike was in a frenzy. Ashleigh was the worst, until her mother finally persuaded her to go back to the Griffen farm and rest.

Samantha walked up to Mrs. Griffen as Ashleigh was heading up the drive in her car. Elaine Griffen shook her blond head. She didn't look old enough to be the mother of a bride, Samantha thought, and Ashleigh wasn't even her eldest child. "I don't know how I'm going to get her to calm down," she said worriedly. "Wedding jitters can be bad enough, but all this nonsense with Brad. I've known him since he was about fourteen, and he hasn't changed. But you'd think he and his wife would have a little consideration, with Ashleigh's wedding tomorrow."

"They don't think about anyone but themselves," Samantha said, then added, "Is there anything I can do to help, Mrs. Griffen?"

Ashleigh's mother smiled her appreciation. "Thanks, Sammy, but believe it or not, we have things pretty much under control. Ashleigh and Mike are just too strung out right now to realize it. I'll see you at the rehearsal dinner tonight."

"Tor and I will be there."

Saturday couldn't have been more gorgeous. The sky was a brilliant blue, and they had a reprieve from the normally hot, humid July weather. The air was clear and the temperature in the seventies. Samantha, Jilly, Linda, and Caroline waited in the living room of the Reese house for the bride to arrive. Ashleigh and Mike would be married in one of the tents under a huge arched trellis of flowers. More flowers were massed up and down the aisle and all around the tent, which was already filled with seated wedding guests. Through the open windows of the living room came the strains of classical music played by a professional pianist and violinist. Mike, his father, and his best man, Chad McGowan, an old friend who had worked with Mike when he'd first begun training, were in the den, awaiting Ashleigh's arrival, too. Ashleigh's brother, Rory, and Tor were acting as ushers in the tent.

The bridesmaids exchanged nervous and excited smiles. Caroline smoothed the skirt of her rose-colored gown and said to the others, "Do you believe she still wouldn't even let *me* see her dress?"

"I'll bet it's beautiful!" Linda said. "And I think I'd want to keep my dress secret, too, when and if I ever get married."

"Oh, you will," Jilly said.

"Right now that's not one of my priorities, but I'm sure happy for Ashleigh and Mike. I always knew they'd get married someday. They're perfect for each other."

Samantha had gone to the window and peeked out. "Here she comes!" The others hurried to the window to look out. Ashleigh's father pulled up in the Chrysler Ashleigh had been awarded the year before for riding Pride to victory in the Kentucky Derby. He climbed out and opened the rear door. Mrs. Griffen hurried around from the passenger side. Mr. Griffen reached out a hand to Ashleigh, and she carefully emerged to stand by the side of the car as her mother bent to smooth the folds of her dress. All the girls gasped. Ashleigh's gown was stunning—a simple ivory satin with tight chiffon sleeves and a full sweep of ankle-length skirt. The scooped neck of the gown and the base of the skirt were delicately embroidered with pale pink roses. Ashleigh had pulled her long, dark hair on top of her head and crowned it with a garland of roses that matched those embroidered on her gown. From the garland a long, lacy veil frothed out like a misty halo and fell all the way to the ground.

The young women turned as Ashleigh and her parents made their way inside. They all exclaimed over her dress and how beautiful she looked. Ashleigh smiled, looking just a little nervous, but she was glowing.

Caroline hurried over and gave her sister a kiss on the cheek. "I never thought you'd be getting married before me," she said teasingly, "incurable tomboy that you were."

"She sure doesn't look like a tomboy today," Linda said. "Wait till Mike sees you, Ash!"

A pretty flush of color tinted Ashleigh's cheeks. Mrs. Griffen handed Ashleigh her bouquet, a long spray of roses and baby's breath. "Are you ready?" she asked her daughter with a smile, although Samantha could see there was a mist of tears in her eyes. When Ashleigh nodded happily, Mr. Griffen went to the back room to let Mike know. The groom and best man would leave through the rear door and wait in front of the tent under the flowered arch. Ashleigh and her attendants would leave through the front door and follow a white carpet laid across the grass to the rear of the tent.

They all knew what to do. They had gone through all the steps at the rehearsal session the night before. Caroline went to the front of the line, followed by Linda, Jilly, and Samantha. Mr. and Mrs. Griffen walked to either side of Ashleigh. "Ready?" Mr. Griffen asked quietly, looking down at his daughter.

"I'm ready," Ashleigh said with happy conviction.

Caroline started forward at a slow, measured walk, with the others following. As they rounded the corner of the house they could see the crowded tent and Mike, Chad, and the justice of the peace standing under the flowered arch. Caroline paused. Suddenly the air rang with the chords of "Here Comes the Bride." The guests, in suits and elegant summer dresses, all quickly stood and turned to watch the wedding party.

Samantha had to swallow back her nervousness as she approached the aisle. So many people were watching her. She prayed she didn't trip and fall. If she was this nervous, what must Ashleigh be feeling? She saw Rory, who was her own age, standing on one side of the aisle. He looked very handsome and grown-up in his tux. Tor stood on the other side of the aisle, also looking very handsome. He gave Samantha a smile. She smiled back and felt a little less nervous.

Then they were moving down the aisle. Samantha saw many familiar faces, friends of Ashleigh and Mike, people they knew from the racing and breeding industry. She saw her father and Beth. Her father was gazing at her with a proud smile. A row in front of them, she saw the Townsends. She was glad to see Mr. Townsend, but why couldn't Brad and Lavinia have stayed home? Ashleigh had been forced to invite them out of politeness, but they should have had the sense to know they weren't welcome.

Caroline had reached the end of the aisle and turned to the left. The other bridesmaids followed and lined up beside her, facing the arch. They all turned to watch Ashleigh and her parents approach and stop before the justice of the peace, Mike, and Chad. Mike looked great in his white tux. His gaze caught Ashleigh's, and they smiled. Ashleigh's father lifted her veil, kissed her cheek, and stepped back. Ashleigh kissed her mother, then Ashleigh took her place beside Mike and handed Caroline her bouquet. Mike and Ashleigh exchanged another loving look before the justice of the peace began the ceremony.

Samantha listened to Ashleigh and Mike's softly spoken responses and vows, wondering if she would one day be uttering similar words. They had written part of the ceremony themselves, and it was beautiful. Samantha's eyes blurred with sentimental tears. Through it all, Ashleigh and Mike's eyes met and held. It was obvious how much they loved each other and how much they meant the words they were saying. Mike took Ashleigh's hand and placed the ring on her fourth finger. She did the same with his ring. Then the justice of the peace cried jubilantly, "I pronounce you husband and wife. You may kiss the bride!"

It was a long and happy kiss. When the bride and

groom turned toward the gathered guests, their faces were wreathed with smiles of joy and relief.

Caroline handed Ashleigh her bouquet, the musicians struck the first chords of the wedding march, the guests stood, and Ashleigh and Mike started back down the aisle as husband and wife.

AFTER THE GUESTS HAD FILED PAST THE BRIDE AND GROOM, Samantha took her turn hugging Ashleigh. "It was so beautiful, Ash. I'm so happy for you!"

"I'm pretty happy myself," Ashleigh said, glancing over to Mike, who was smilingly receiving his own congratulations from the wedding party.

A moment later they moved across to a tree-shaded paddock near the barn for the formal wedding photographs. Ashleigh and Mike had decided that they wanted their special horses in at least a few of the photos. Len, smiling broadly and wearing the black suit he saved for special occasions, supervised as the two extra grooms Mike had hired for the day led out Jazzman, Pride, Wonder and Mr. Wonderful, and Fleet Goddess and her foal, Precocious.

The older horses were used to having their pictures taken—they'd certainly had enough taken in the winner's circle. The foals, however, were more interested in checking out each other and their new surroundings. The wedding party was in stitches watching their antics. They seemed set on frustrating the photographer. Precocious decided the roses in Ashleigh's headpiece looked enticing, and just as the photographer said "Ready," she reached up her head to take a bite. As another photo was being snapped Mr. Wonderful decided the view behind Ashleigh and Mike was more interesting. He swung around, and the photographer got a perfect shot of the foal's rump.

Finally all the photos were taken, and they returned to the huge tents for the champagne toast to the bride and groom and the wedding meal. Guests were gathered on the lawns or under the striped canopy talking; others had taken seats at the dozens of white-linen-covered tables. Waiters and waitresses circulated with glasses of champagne.

"You look more relaxed than when I saw you heading down the aisle," Tor said to Samantha with a chuckle. "It was nice, wasn't it?"

"It sure was! Didn't Ashleigh look beautiful?"

"So did you," Tor said, looking down at her.

Samantha immediately felt a flush rising up her cheeks. "Thanks," she murmured. But she knew the dress was becoming, and Caroline had done Samantha's hair for her, pulling it to one side so that a cascade of curls fell down along Samantha's cheek.

Yvonne and Gregg joined them. "What a gorgeous wedding!" Yvonne exclaimed. "And they both look so happy! They've got an incredible band, too." She motioned to a third tent, where a portable dance floor had been placed and an excellent local country-rock group was beginning to set up their speakers and instruments. "The only bummer is that Lavinia and Brad came," Yvonne added. "God, they've got nerve! How can they even show their faces after what they've done to Ashleigh? I thought they'd have the decency to leave after the ceremony, but they're still here." Yvonne jerked her head sideways to where they stood.

Lavinia was playing the social butterfly now. She and Brad were moving through the crowd, pausing to talk to the more successful breeders and racing people. "I'm going to do my best to ignore them," Samantha said, "though it won't be easy. Just listen to her."

Lavinia's marble-mouthed tones carried above the general murmur of the guests' conversation. She was standing a few yards away, talking to the young wife of a successful Lexington breeder. "Rather a sweet wedding," Lavinia was saying, making it sound more like an insult. "I've always found it strange, though, that my father-in-law turned over a half-interest in Wonder to her. It's not like she did anything to deserve it. She was only a *groom*."

"From what I've heard, she was more than that," the other young woman responded. "She and Charlie Burke turned the filly around and made her a champion. I think your father-in-law had reason to be grateful."

Lavinia sniffed. Samantha had heard enough. "Let's get away from her," she said. The caterers had been setting up the buffet on a long table to the side of the tent. Beside it was another table, where one of the caterer's staff was serving up glasses of champagne. Other uniformed waiters were standing behind the buffet table, lifting the covers off the variety of dishes and preparing to carve freshly roasted beef and ham.

Samantha, Tor, Yvonne, and Gregg drifted with the rest of the crowd toward the buffet. Ashleigh had left the seating informal. She and Mike and their immediate families sat at the head table, but the balance of the wedding party and guests could select their own seating. Samantha saw Linda and Jilly motion from one of the tables. When they'd filled their plates, Samantha, Tor, Yvonne, and Gregg joined them. Jilly's husband, Craig, arrived with his laden plate a moment later.

"What's this?" Jilly said to him teasingly. "You'll put on two pounds this afternoon alone. Looks like you'll be spending tomorrow morning in the sweat room."

Craig laughed. "I'm entitled to splurge once in a while, and this food is too good to refuse."

"Okay," Jilly said to Linda, "our turn to get some food."

Linda hadn't brought a date, but she didn't seem the least disturbed that she was the only one in the wedding party who was alone. Caroline and her husband-to-be, Justin McGowan, Chad's brother, were seated at the table with Ashleigh and Mike.

As Jilly and Linda headed off to the buffet, Chad McGowan arrived at the table. "Room for one more?" he asked.

"Sure," Craig answered, motioning to an empty seat. Samantha introduced Chad to Yvonne and Gregg.

"I can't believe what Mike and his father have done with the farm," Chad said. "It's just incredible when you think that Mike and I started with just two horses when we were juniors in high school—of course, one of the horses was Jazzman." Chad grinned. "He earned plenty for Mike."

"Are you still working with horses?" Samantha asked.

Chad shook his head. "I ride once in a while, and go to the track when I can, but I've got a dull old office job now. I work for a brokerage firm, selling stocks and bonds. Actually, I've been giving Mike and Mr. Reese some advice about investments."

Linda and Jilly had returned to the table. Jilly had more willpower than her husband and had filled her plate with only the low-calorie offerings.

"How long are you going to be around?" Chad asked Linda.

"For the summer; then I'm heading off to graduate school." She giggled at Chad's expression. "Yeah, can you imagine *me* going to graduate school? I sure wasn't much of a student in high school, but I've really gotten interested in sports therapy."

Samantha knew Linda had been a star tennis player in high school and college. For years she had also helped her trainer father work his horses and was a skilled horsewoman. Linda definitely had the background for working with sports injuries.

They all chatted happily as they finished their meal. The band was playing some mellow background music. As waiters came to clear the tables, the band picked up the beat, and it wasn't long before people were out on the dance floor. Samantha and Tor and Yvonne and Gregg soon joined them. Samantha saw her father and Beth dancing to one of the slower songs. Earlier she'd noticed them wandering around through the crowd, with their arms linked. She was determined not to think about them and let it ruin her afternoon. She was having too good a time.

An hour later Ashleigh and Mike cut the cake, and pieces were distributed to the guests. Then Chad, looking a little self conscious, stood and made a toast to the bride and groom. While the toast was being given, Samantha noticed Charlie and Mr. Townsend standing in the far corner of the tent talking. Samantha hoped Charlie was giving Mr. Townsend a full accounting of what Lavinia and Brad had been up to while he was away. Then Lavinia joined the two of them. Charlie frowned deeply at something Lavinia said. Mr. Townsend responded with a comment to Lavinia. Samantha was too far away to hear the conversation, but a moment later Charlie turned on his heel and strode off.

He walked up to the table, still scowling. "What did she say?" Samantha asked quietly.

Charlie shook his head. "Nothing I care to repeat." Then he added, "Townsend tells me they're racing Lord Ainsley in the Haskell Invitational at Monmouth the first of August."

130

"So he's recovered," Samantha said. "That's a Grade one race."

"Yup. That should set him up for the Whitney at the end of the month."

"At least he won't be running against Pride in the Haskell," Samantha said. "Maybe Brad and Lavinia will leave us alone."

"Don't count on it." Charlie's jaw was tight, and his face looked gray.

"You look upset," Samantha said.

Charlie just shook his head. "Don't worry about me."

The band was playing again, and Tor asked Samantha to dance.

When they returned to the table, Charlie was still scowling. Samantha looked at him with concern. She thought of calling her father.

Then suddenly Charlie groaned, clutched his chest, and bent over. Samantha reached for him. "Charlie!" she cried in horror when she saw his grimace of pain and watched the remaining color drain from his face. She grabbed his arm, trying to steady him. Tor rushed to her aide, supporting Charlie's shoulders with his arm. "Help!" Samantha shouted above the din of the crowd. "Somebody help!"

People turned and stared. "I think he's had a heart attack!" Tor cried. "We need help and a doctor!"

Samantha looked around in desperation. Charlie was collapsing in her and Tor's arms. He wasn't even groaning out his pain anymore, which made Samantha feel even more frightened and anxious.

One of the guests rushed forward. "I'm a doctor,"

131

he said with authority. His eyes were on Charlie. "Let's make him comfortable," he said to Tor and Samantha. "Somebody call an ambulance." As Mike hurried over to help, they gently eased Charlie to the ground. Mr. Reese rushed off to the house. Someone else hurried over with a blanket. Charlie's breathing was labored; his eyes were closed and his face was a deathly shade. Samantha felt her own heart contract with fear.

She glanced across to Ashleigh's shocked face. "What can I do?" Ashleigh cried.

The doctor was concentrating all his attention on Charlie and didn't respond. He'd loosened Charlie's tie and collar and was feeling his pulse. A young woman pushed through the crowd. "I've had emergency training," she said to the doctor. He nodded, and she knelt beside him, following his instructions.

"Anyone know his medical history?" the doctor asked. "Any history of heart trouble?"

"Yes," Ashleigh answered hoarsely. "He was having trouble a couple of years ago, but he's never had a heart attack. Charlie doesn't talk about his health . . . he doesn't like people fussing."

Mr. Reese hurried up. "The ambulance is on its way."

Samantha gripped Tor's hand. She prayed it wouldn't be too late for Charlie, who seemed to have lost consciousness. She wanted to pretend this wasn't happening. She glanced around the circle of shocked faces—her father, Clay Townsend, Hank, Len, Linda, Ken Maddock, Jilly and Craig, Yvonne. They'd all been close to Charlie. Maybe, like Samantha, they'd all thought he would go on forever and ever. At the fringe of the crowd she saw Lavinia and Brad, but she couldn't read their expressions.

There were murmurs of distress from the wedding guests, but everyone stayed back, giving the doctor and Charlie room. Finally in the distance Samantha heard the distinctive two-tone siren of the ambulance. Charlie was breathing, but he was struggling for each breath. "Please be all right," Samantha whispered fervently.

The ambulance braked to a halt in the drive, and the ambulance crew hurried forward with a wheeled stretcher, an oxygen mask, and other medical equipment. Under the doctor's instructions they worked quickly and professionally. Within minutes they had lifted Charlie to the stretcher, oxygen mask in place, and were wheeling him toward the open back of the ambulance. The doctor climbed in behind the stretcher. Then the siren sounded again as they sped up the drive and down the highway toward Lexington.

Samantha clutched Tor's arm and stared at the departing vehicle. "Charlie looked so awful!" she cried. "Oh, Tor, I can't stand to think of Charlie dying! I knew something was wrong. I should have called my father, or Len, or Mr. Reese—"

"Stop, Sammy," Tor said with a catch in his voice. "Don't blame yourself. You couldn't have known he was that ill. And he's a fighter. There's a chance he'll pull through."

Yvonne rushed over and hugged Samantha. Her brown eyes were filled with tears. All around was a low murmur of stunned conversation and dazed and saddened faces. No one seemed to know what to do. Ashleigh had her head on Mike's shoulder, and tears streamed down her cheeks. Samantha went over to the older girl. "Oh, Ash," she cried, trying to control her own voice. "He'll be all right, Ash. I know he's going to be all right." Samantha tried desperately to convince herself that was true.

Ashleigh choked back a sob. "I should have paid more attention—made him take care of himself. He never did."

"He wouldn't let anyone coddle him," Mike said. "You know that." But he looked as broken up as Ashleigh.

"I want to go to the hospital," Ashleigh told him. "I want to be with Charlie."

"We'll go," Mike said. "Let's change out of these clothes first."

They turned toward the house. Ashleigh's family went with them.

The remaining members of the wedding party stood uncertainly in the tent and exchanged stunned glances. Samantha was vaguely aware of the guests quietly departing, the sound of car engines starting and tires crunching on gravel.

"I wish there was something we could do," Jilly murmured, wiping the tears from her cheeks. "Charlie is the most incredible man—gruff and short-tempered, maybe, but he's done so much for all of us, and he's the best trainer I've ever known. He doesn't just train horses—he gets into their minds and personalities. He understands them and works with their special problems, and that's what makes horses win. God, I'll miss him if he doesn't pull through! And poor Ashleigh and Mike."

"Did he say anything about not feeling well?" Linda asked.

"No," Samantha answered, "but when he came back to the table, he didn't look good. I should have told someone, but then—" She couldn't get out the rest of the words.

Her father walked over and put his arm around her shoulders. "Oh, Dad!" she cried.

"We'll just have to hope for the best, Sammy," he said somberly. "I'm going to drive Len to the hospital. He's taking it pretty hard. Will you be all right?"

Samantha nodded.

"Stay at the Reeses'. Someone will call from the hospital as soon as there's news."

"We'll all stay," Tor said, "if Mr. Reese doesn't mind."

"I'm sure he doesn't." Mr. McLean gave Samantha's shoulders another squeeze, then he and Beth headed toward the drive, where Len was standing with Hank and Ken Maddock. Gradually, still dazed and shocked, the rest of them moved inside to wait for news.

12

AN HOUR LATER THEY WERE STILL WAITING ANXIOUSLY IN the Reeses' living room. Outside, the caterers were cleaning up. The band had long gone, as had the guests, including Lavinia and Brad, who had departed quickly. Mr. Townsend had remained behind for a while, talking to Mr. Griffen, his former breeding manager, and Mr. Reese. He had looked very upset.

"I know the problems with Lavinia and Brad were getting to Charlie," Jilly said miserably to the others. "The strain must have been too much for him." She shook her head and covered her face with her hands.

"I don't have any love for them either," Mr. Reese said, "but in fairness, we can't jump to conclusions. Charlie's an old man, and he's had heart problems in the past."

"Lavinia did say something to him today that upset him," Samantha murmured. The others turned

136

to look at her. "But I don't know what. He wouldn't tell me. Don't say anything to Ashleigh," she added quickly. "She's already worried enough."

"You're right," Jilly said. "It wouldn't do any good now."

"I just hope he pulls through," Samantha whispered. All she could think of was how devastated Ashleigh would be if he didn't—how nothing would seem the same without the crusty old trainer. Samantha glanced around the room and saw the same thought echoed on everyone's face.

The phone shrilled from the table by the door. They all jumped. Mr. Reese stepped over quickly to answer it. "Mike, yes, what's the news?" he said. The others stared tensely in his direction.

Mr. Reese frowned as he listened, then nodded grimly. "I'll tell the others. How's Ashleigh holding up? Yes, I think that's a good idea. See you in a little while."

He hung up the phone and turned. "Charlie . . ." His voice caught. "Charlie passed away a few minutes ago."

"No!" Samantha cried, covering her mouth with her hand. Tor's arm went around her shoulders. Jilly broke down in sobs, and Craig tried to comfort her. The others stared in shocked disbelief.

"I really thought he would make it," Mr. Griffen said in a dazed tone. "Charlie was such a fighter."

Mr. Reese continued unsteadily. "He had a massive coronary. The doctors couldn't do much but try to make him comfortable. Ashleigh, Mike, and Len

were with him. Mike said Charlie regained consciousness for a few minutes. He couldn't talk, but at least
he knew they were there." Mr. Reese stared down at
his feet, trying to regain his composure.

"How's Ashleigh?" Mrs. Griffen asked worriedly.

"Not good. Mike didn't sound too good either.
Ian's driving them and Len home."

"She and Charlie were so close," Mrs. Griffen murmured. "She looked up to him so. When I remember . . ."
She broke off in a sob, and her husband held her. Linda
and Yvonne looked on the verge of tears, too. The men
all seemed to be struggling with their emotions.

"We have to remember he had a good, long life,"
Mr. Griffen said, "and think of all the good he's done
for others. He's sure going to be missed."

In quiet voices they spoke of their memories of
Charlie. It helped ease the grief, but to Samantha it
still didn't seem possible that she'd never see the
gruff old trainer again. She wanted desperately to
pretend that Charlie's death was just a horrible
dream, and that she'd wake up in a moment to find
him sitting there in the room with them.

When Ashleigh and Mike arrived, followed by
Len, Mr. McLean, and Beth, Ashleigh looked on the
verge of collapse. Her face was white as a sheet; her
eyes red rimmed. Mike and Len didn't look much
better. Mrs. Griffen hurried over to her daughter, and
after a few whispered words from Mike helped
Ashleigh from the room. Caroline quickly followed.

Mike looked completely drained and went to the
sofa to sit and drop his head into his hands. "Ashleigh's

had too much to deal with," Mike said. "We both have—from the heights to the depths in one day."

Mike's father walked over and laid a comforting hand on his son's shoulder.

"I think we should all go," Yvonne said softly.

Mike shook his head. "No, stay. I'd rather have company, and I know Ash will want her close friends around. She just needs to pull herself together. She cared so much for Charlie, and with everything else that's been going on . . ."

A few minutes later Ashleigh returned to the room to sit beside Mike. She had obviously freshened up, but she still looked pale and shaken. Beth and Mrs. Griffen brought out food that no one had much interest in eating. Samantha was too upset to even notice what an active part Beth was taking. Len, looking older than he had a few hours before, told them that he had a copy of Charlie's will. "He gave it to me a couple of months ago for safekeeping. He must have guessed the old ticker wasn't what it should be," Len said sadly. "Never complained, though."

"We'll have to make funeral arrangements," Mr. Reese said.

Len shook his grizzled gray head. "Charlie told me he didn't want any fancy funeral . . . just to have his ashes thrown over one of the pastures . . . where he could be close to his horses."

"I want him to have a memorial service," Ashleigh said firmly. "Charlie wouldn't want anything flowery, but to recap his career, remind the racing world what he's done . . . not that it would make up for losing him." Ashleigh turned to Mike and took his hand. She looked ready to break down in tears again, but she bit her lip.

"I don't suppose Charlie would object to that," Len responded. "Lord knows, he deserves it."

During the next days, everyone tried to carry on. The horses still had to be worked, preparations made for the trip to Saratoga, and arrangements made for Charlie's memorial service. Life on the training farm went on, but everyone seemed to be going through the motions in a daze.

News of Charlie's death swept through the racing industry. The phone rang constantly. All the racing papers carried obituaries and glowing tributes to Charlie's years in racing.

Ashleigh had gradually recovered from her shock, but she certainly didn't have the glow of a newlywed. "It helps to know how loved and respected Charlie was," Ashleigh confided to Samantha. "But I miss him so much! And how can I ever fill his shoes? I always counted on his advice, and if I did something wrong, you know he'd be sure to tell me. How am I going to get Pride ready for the Whitney without him?"

"Ash, you can do it," Samantha said firmly. "You learned a lot from Charlie, and you've got Mike or my father to give you advice if you're not sure."

"I suppose you're right. Mike's been wonderful. This hasn't been a very good start to our marriage, but in a way, I think it's made us even closer. I know he'll be there if I need him. There's just so much to do this week, and I keep expecting to see Charlie walk out of the barn . . ."

"I know," Samantha said, her voice catching. She'd experienced the same thing, and it hurt every time she reminded herself that Charlie wouldn't walk out of the barn again. It brought back sharp and painful memories of the horrible days after her mother's death.

"What frightens me, too," Ashleigh said, "is that now I'm going to have to deal with Lavinia and Brad alone—me against them."

"You won't be alone! You've got Mike, and me, and Jilly." Samantha wasn't about to tell Ashleigh that she had her own fears.

"I think I'm going to put off leaving for Saratoga, though," Ashleigh said. "I just don't feel ready, and we have Charlie's memorial service to arrange." They were all supposed to leave for Saratoga the first of August. It had been planned for months.

Len walked up and heard the last part of their conversation. He shook his head. "The last thing Charlie would want you to do is put off the Saratoga trip," he said. "You go up and make Charlie proud. The memorial service can wait. In fact, it might be a nice idea to have it up there, where he spent nearly every summer season. We'll be spreading Charlie's ashes here before we leave. That'll be enough for him."

On Wednesday evening, Ashleigh rode Wonder over the pastures with the small urn containing Charlie's ashes. It seemed only fitting that the mare

Charlie and Ashleigh had believed in when no one else had should be there for a last good-bye. Ashleigh had chosen a spot that overlooked the spreading acres of Whitebrook, the barns, and the training oval. Charlie could have an endless view of the Thoroughbreds he'd loved, and the place where they were trained.

Samantha watched with Mike, Mr. Reese, Len, and her father as the horse and rider made their way up the grassy slope of the pasture. The last rays of sunlight glinted off Wonder's copper coat and the dark strands of Ashleigh's hair. At the top of the rise, Ashleigh stopped and turned Wonder. She spoke to the horse, and Wonder cocked her ears back, listening, then seemed to bob her elegant head. Ashleigh put Wonder into a slow and graceful canter, and as the two of them circled the crest of the hill, Ashleigh let Charlie's ashes drift behind them to settle on the lush grass.

Samantha felt the warm wetness of tears streaming down her cheeks and choked back a sob. A moment later she felt a hand on her shoulder and looked up to see her father wiping at his own eyes. At that moment Samantha felt a touch of the old bond with her father that Beth had seemed to rupture.

Ashleigh was sobbing, too, as she and Wonder returned down the slope. She stopped Wonder beside the others and dismounted, then reached up to press her tear-stained cheek against the mare's silky neck. "We won't let anyone forget him, will we, girl? I'm going to take your son up to Saratoga and win the

Whitney. I'm going to do it for Charlie. I'm going to make sure Brad and Lavinia get exactly what they deserve! Wouldn't that make Charlie happy!"

The beautiful mare whickered softly and gently bobbed her head as if she shared Ashleigh's feelings. Then she craned her head around and lovingly lipped Ashleigh's hair.

When Samantha rode Pride out for his last workout before Saratoga a few days later, Ashleigh stood alone at the rail, looking slightly overwhelmed by the responsibility of being totally in charge of Pride's training. It seemed so strange to Samantha not to see Charlie standing nearby, pushing back his felt hat as he squinted out to the track. But Samantha knew Ashleigh could do it. Charlie had taught her well.

Despite Ashleigh's worried frown as she watched, the workout was going perfectly, and Samantha hoped that would buoy Ashleigh's confidence. Samantha set Pride down to breeze out the last quarter mile as Ashleigh had instructed. Pride's galloping strides ate up the track. When they swept past the marker post, Samantha knew their fractions for the quarter had been excellent. She patted Pride's neck and praised him as she turned him back to the gap.

Ashleigh was no longer alone. Mr. Townsend and Lavinia were with her. Samantha clenched her teeth in absolute fury to see Lavinia at Whitebrook again. As Samantha rode up she heard Mr. Townsend say sadly to Ashleigh, "We're all going to miss Charlie. He was a good man. His death was a tragedy at any time, but I'm so sorry it happened at your wedding."

Ashleigh nodded. "Yes, but Mike and I are handling it. I know Charlie wouldn't have wanted things to happen the way they did."

"Of course not," Mr. Townsend agreed.

"I *told* him he was too old to train and that he should retire gracefully," Lavinia said.

Samantha's breath caught as she digested Lavinia's words. That must have been what Lavinia had told Charlie at the wedding reception. The comment must have been the last straw for the old man, who was already under pressure.

"You really don't have any choice but to put Maddock in charge," Lavinia told her father-in-law in sweet tones, "and have Pride brought to Townsend Acres. All along Brad and I have thought that was the sensible thing to do—"

Ashleigh cut her short. "I'm perfectly capable of training Pride myself, Lavinia. I *have* been training him right along—with a certain amount of success!"

"You've only assisted. You don't have the experience or knowledge—"

Now Mr. Townsend interrupted. "I have every confidence in Ashleigh's abilities," he told Lavinia sharply. "She knows Pride. She knows what works best. I have no intention of changing the current arrangement. We did that in the past, with disastrous results. And Pride just put in a very impressive workout."

Samantha knew, when she saw the expression on Lavinia's face, that Lavinia wasn't going to let it end

144

there. She and Brad would wait until Clay Townsend wasn't around.

Mr. Townsend turned to Ashleigh. "If I don't see you before, I'll see you in Saratoga. You'll be leaving Saturday . . ."

As Mr. Townsend and Ashleigh discussed travel plans, Lavinia strode off toward her Cherokee. Samantha dismounted, pulled up the stirrups, and began walking Pride. A moment later, when Mr. Townsend left, too, she spoke encouragingly to Ashleigh. "It's going to be all right, Ash. Mr. Townsend's definitely on your side."

That night at dinner, Samantha's father gave her another jarring surprise. "Beth's going to be coming up to Saratoga with us," he said. "She has some vacation time and hasn't been to Saratoga before. I think she'll enjoy it, don't you?"

Samantha froze with her fork halfway to her mouth. She'd been looking forward to a month *without* Beth constantly hanging on her father and getting all his attention.

"Maybe *she'll* have a good time," Samantha muttered angrily. "But *I* sure won't."

Her father frowned at her. "Sammy," he said with a touch of anger in his voice, "I know you're upset about Charlie—we all are——but don't you think you're carrying this animosity toward Beth a little too far? She goes out of her way to be pleasant to you. I can't for the life of me understand why you're so hostile toward her. Don't you think you're behaving childishly?"

"Childishly!" Samantha thought of all the responsibilities she'd assumed since her mother had died. She remembered how she had held her father up emotionally when she was aching herself. How could he think she was acting childishly? She had had to grow up a lot faster than most kids her age. "I am *not* being childish! How do you think I feel? She's here all the time. She acts like she owns the cottage. She tries to tell me how to do things when I've been doing them perfectly well for four years! She's not my mother and never will be! Maybe she's got you fooled, but—"

"That's enough, Sammy!" her father said angrily. "You're totally off base!"

"No, I'm not! I don't like her. But you don't care what I think anymore. It's just Beth . . . Beth . . . Beth!"

"That's not true, Samantha, and you know it!"

"It *is* true!" Samantha shouted back, close to tears. "When was the last time *we* did anything together? If you really cared about me, you wouldn't bring her!"

Samantha knew her outburst had upset her father, but she also saw the stubborn tightness of his jaw as he stared across the table at her. "Beth is coming to Saratoga. She's made all the arrangements and is looking forward to it. I'm not going to disappoint her by asking her to change her plans now. You're just going to have to live with it, Sammy."

Samantha pushed back her chair and rushed from the room. She was furious, and hurt beyond belief that her father hadn't seemed to listen to a word she'd been saying. He'd jumped to Beth's defense instead of his own daughter's! Her emotions were stretched to the limit trying to deal with Charlie's death. She just couldn't take any more! She threw herself on the bed and sobbed. Her father didn't even come up to see if she was all right.

Tor picked Samantha up at ten the next morning. She hadn't slept well. Her eyes felt scratchy, and her thoughts were a muddle. Everything seemed to be falling apart. But that morning she had an appointment to take her driving test in Lexington. She had had to wait weeks to get the appointment and didn't want to cancel it, especially since they were leaving for Saratoga the next day.

Tor looked at her with concern as she got in the car. "Are you all right?" he asked.

Samantha nodded. She wasn't going to tell him about her argument with her father. They'd already gotten in one fight over Samantha's feelings about Beth.

Tor reached across the seat and squeezed her hand. "It's been a horrible few days," he said understandingly. "Maybe getting your license will cheer you up a little."

But an hour later, when Samantha parked Tor's car in the Department of Motor Vehicles lot, she knew she hadn't passed the test. She'd forgotten to signal for a turn at a stop sign, and that had so unsettled her that she'd totally messed up trying to parallel park and had had to try three times before she maneuvered the car into the slot.

Samantha looked over to the driving inspector in

the passenger seat, and he shook his head. He saw her disappointment. "Sorry," he said, "but I can't pass you."

"I know." She pressed her lips together to keep them from trembling. Her eyes were really stinging now, but she held herself in control until she met Tor outside the building.

"I didn't pass," she said, and now the tears streamed down her cheeks.

Tor quickly put his arm around her shoulders. "Oh, Sammy, that's a bummer, but you don't have to take it so hard. You'll have another chance. A lot of people fail on their first try. You get so nervous, you make silly mistakes."

Samantha swallowed. She wasn't going to tell Tor that her failure was due to more than nerves.

"After we get back from Saratoga," Tor said encouragingly, "I'll take you out for some more practice sessions, and you can make another appointment. I know you'll pass."

Samantha nodded, but at the moment she couldn't feel optimistic about anything.

At least Samantha didn't have to put up with Beth during the drive to Saratoga. Her father and Beth were driving up in the McLeans' car. Samantha, Ashleigh, Mike, and Len went in the huge horse van with Pride and a number of Mike's horses. Mike had hired another groom to help. He and Len rode in the back with the horses. The following weekend Tor would be vanning Sierra up.

They left at dawn and arrived at the upstate New York track in the early-evening hours, stopping only once for gas and to check the horses. Mike had reserved his own row of stabling. Pride, as usual, went into the Townsend Acres stabling one row over, but this time he had a roomy end stall. Hank had seen to that, and Lavinia and Brad were in Monmouth, New Jersey, anyway. Lord Ainsley had raced that afternoon in the Haskell Invitational.

They were all anxious to hear the outcome of the Haskell, and they soon got the details from the backside staff. Lord Ainsley had won it easily. "I've got it on video," Hank told Ashleigh, "if you want to take a look at it."

"I sure do."

After the horses were settled, with the new groom keeping an eye on them, they went to the lounge area provided for the backside staff and Hank ran the video. All Samantha could think as she watched the race replay was that Lavinia and Brad finally ought to be happy. There was really no contest. Lord Ainsley sat just off the leaders into the far turn, then effortlessly drew away to a two-length victory.

"Of course, he wasn't running against that much," Hank said. "There were some decent horses in the field, but none of them compare to Pride."

"I guess there's no question now that he and Pride will be matching up in the Whitney," Ashleigh said. "I wonder what sneaky tricks Lavinia and Brad have planned to make sure Lord Ainsley wins? Oh, God, I wish Charlie were here!"

13

THEIR FIRST WEEK AT SARATOGA WAS FAIRLY PEACEFUL since Brad and Lavinia weren't there yet. They would be bringing Lord Ainsley up the following weekend. Samantha enjoyed the quiet while it lasted, and she loved the old track, with its turreted grandstands and tree-shaded grounds.

She worked Pride several times on the track with Ashleigh and Mike watching. Pride was gathering a lot of attention, and Ashleigh was slowly gaining more confidence, but they all missed Charlie. Many times Samantha caught herself looking for the old trainer, expecting to see him with stopwatch in hand along the rail or gazing in over the stall door when she was grooming Pride. Ashleigh and Pride were both doing well, though, and that helped to ease the sense of loss.

The only real problem Samantha had was that she rarely saw her father alone. Beth came bubbling out of

150

her room every morning to make a nutritious breakfast for them; she did the laundry and organized their social schedule—buzzing around like a happy little homemaker. She even came to the track to watch the early-morning workouts, so Samantha didn't have that time alone with her father either. Since their argument, they hadn't discussed his relationship with Beth. Several times Samantha saw a look of concern on his face, but they never seemed to have an opportunity for a private talk. Samantha couldn't wait for Tor to arrive.

When he finally drove the van carrying Sierra onto the backside the following Saturday, Samantha rushed out to meet him. And he had a surprise for her. Yvonne jumped down from the passenger seat with a huge grin.

Samantha gave her a hug. "I'm so glad to see you, but why didn't you tell me you were coming?"

"I only decided yesterday," Yvonne explained. "Cisco was doing so well, I decided I could give him a rest and come up and see Sierra and Pride race."

Tor had stepped around the van and hugged Samantha, too. "It'll be like last year, with all of us together."

"Let's hope it *ends* better than last year," Samantha said. The previous year Pride had lost the Travers and the Townsends decided to take him back to Townsend Acres.

"This year Pride is going to win!" Yvonne said confidently.

"I hope! I guess we'd better get Sierra settled. How did he travel?" Samantha asked Tor.

"Fine, but he always does." Tor went to the rear of the van and unlatched the gate. A moment later he led the big liver-chestnut colt out. Sierra lifted his head and surveyed his surroundings, then pranced on his slender legs, glad to be out of the van.

"I've got his stall all set," Samantha said as she gave Sierra's nose a cautious pat. "I've checked out the jump course. If we work him on Monday, he should be set for Wednesday's race."

Tor nodded. As they walked Sierra to his stall, Samantha filled them in on all the news of the past week. "Lavinia and Brad are supposed to arrive today." She scowled.

"They ought to be happy, anyway, after Lord Ainsley won the Haskell," Yvonne said.

"But that doesn't mean they're going to leave us alone—not with Pride and Lord Ainsley matched up in the Whitney."

"Has Mr. Townsend been around?" Tor asked.

"No, unfortunately. Maddock said that he's still in England. No one's sure how long he'll be gone."

"Bummer," said Yvonne.

After they'd settled Sierra and found Mike and Ashleigh, they all left the track and walked down the lovely, shady streets of Saratoga to get pizza. It turned out to be one of their last totally lighthearted meals.

By Monday morning their peace was shattered. Brad and Lavinia were at the rail to watch the morning workouts with a group of their upper-crust friends. The two of them were all smiles, and neither

152

of them could stop bragging about Lord Ainsley's victory. "If we hadn't had to scratch him from the Suburban," Brad said, "I'm sure the outcome would have been different. He's been training more brilliantly than ever."

Samantha pursed her lips as she mounted one of Mike's horses for his workout. She turned the horse and started onto the track. "What a naggy-looking thing," Lavinia said loudly to one of her friends. "You'd never find us running such a poor specimen under Townsend Acres' colors."

Jerk! Samantha thought. Although Blues King, the horse she was riding, wasn't much on looks, he was one of the best sprinters in Mike's stable. Mike had every confidence that he'd win his races.

Samantha had finished the workout by the time Tor rode Sierra out on the turf course. She handed Mike's horse over to Len and went to the rail to watch. Tor had warmed up Sierra and was starting him over the jumps. The big colt scaled the fences effortlessly and galloped smoothly over the grass between them. Tor didn't have to urge him at all, and Samantha felt her hopes rise that they'd do well in Wednesday's steeplechase.

She sensed someone coming up beside her but didn't turn to look. Then she heard Brad's sneering tones. "I heard Mike was trying to run a 'chaser. Things must be getting desperate over there. Have they run out of decent flat-racing stock?" He chuckled snidely and walked away before Samantha could answer.

"We'll show you!" Samantha said under her breath.

Two days later Samantha hoped she would be proved right. She had a knot in her stomach as she watched the first race on the Wednesday card go off. Her eyes were glued to Tor and Sierra as the field headed toward the first fence. It wasn't going to be an easy romp for Sierra—not by a long shot. Several horses in the field had raced against top competition, which Sierra hadn't. But when Sierra and Tor landed off the first fence in the lead, the knot in her stomach gradually loosened. She watched with growing excitement as they kept the lead.

Yvonne started screeching beside her. "Go, Sierra! Keep it up! Boy, am I glad I came!"

Samantha started screaming encouragement herself as they cleared the second-to-last fence and the later closers started moving up through the pack. "Come on! Keep him going, Tor!"

Tor gave Sierra a nudge with his hands, and the big colt accelerated. The others couldn't catch him. Sierra won at odds of 20–1.

"All right!" Mike cheered as he hugged Ashleigh. "We're off to a good start!"

Samantha couldn't wait to see Brad and mention their victory.

They were all in the mood for a celebration that night, but during their meal at a nice restaurant in town a reporter for the *Daily Racing Form* hurried up to their table. "What's this I hear about Pride being scratched from the Whitney?" he asked Ashleigh anxiously.

They all stared at the reporter. "Where did you hear a crazy thing like that?" Ashleigh demanded.

"The rumor's all over the track."

"It's not true," Ashleigh said. "I have absolutely no reason to scratch him. He's in top shape and training beautifully."

The reporter scowled. "That's what I thought. Rumor has it that Townsend Acres has decided not to run part of their entry."

"Darn them!" Ashleigh muttered angrily. "It's a false rumor," she said to the reporter. She balled her napkin and flung it down on her plate. "I'm going to go straighten this out, and I want to check on Pride." She and Mike rose. Mike looked like he was ready to kill somebody.

"I'll go with you," Samantha said quickly.

"No, stay and enjoy your meal, Sammy. You deserve to celebrate."

"I'll be worried sick," Samantha said.

"I'll call you from the track—and Pride should be all right. Len's keeping watch."

Ashleigh and Mike hurried off.

"What those two won't stoop to," Ian McLean said angrily. "To start a rumor that Pride's being scratched. It's totally unethical."

"But I bet they've covered their tracks," Tor said. "No one will be able to prove the rumor started with them."

"Could they scratch Pride from the race?" Beth asked.

"Not without Ashleigh agreeing to it."

"This wouldn't be happening if Charlie or Mr. Townsend was here," Yvonne said.

"I'm sure Lavinia and Brad are trying to take advantage of Ashleigh's youth and inexperience," Mr. McLean said. "Rattle her, if nothing else."

A few minutes later a waiter came to the table to tell Samantha she had a call. She hurried to the phone by the hostess desk.

"Pride's fine," Ashleigh said without preamble. "Though it's a good thing Len was sitting by his stall. Brad and Lavinia brought a bunch of their snotty friends to the backside and wanted to know what Len thought he was doing guarding the stall of a Townsend Acres horse. Len told them he worked for the *other* owner. Lavinia pulled one of her 'lady of the manor' acts, but Len wouldn't budge and they left Pride alone."

"Have you seen them?" Samantha asked.

"Nope—but I can't wait till I do!"

That night when Tor dropped Samantha at the housekeeping apartment Mike had rented for the McLeans, her father was waiting up for her. He was alone, which surprised Samantha even more. Maybe Beth had left early, she thought wickedly.

Her father looked as if he had something to say to her but didn't know how to begin. "Sammy, I need to talk to you. Sit down for a minute." He paused as Samantha sat on the other end of the couch, then continued hesitantly. "I don't like what's happening

156

to us. You're so distant lately, and I know it's partly my fault. I know I've been spending most of my time with Beth and haven't considered your feelings carefully enough. Beth talked to me tonight. She's feeling bad, too. She knows you resent having her around."

Samantha unconsciously stiffened. She didn't like the idea of Beth talking about her, but she wanted to hear what her father had to say.

"I just wanted you to know that you'll always come first with me, Sammy. Please understand, too, that I'll never forget your mother. I will always love her, but she's gone. Beth has become special to me. She can never replace your mother—she doesn't want to. She doesn't want to drive us apart, either. She's decided to go home tomorrow."

Samantha felt a spurt of relief, quickly followed by a twinge of guilt. "She's leaving because of me?"

"Well . . . she thought you might be happier without her here."

Samantha closed her eyes and sighed. A flush rose up her cheeks. This was what she'd wanted—for Beth to go away. Why did she suddenly feel like a childish brat who made other people miserable unless she got her own way?

Her father reached over and took her hand. "Sammy, I'm finally able to see how hard it's been for you—"

Now Samantha really felt guilty. "Dad, it's my fault, too. I wouldn't give Beth a chance. Since Mom died, it's just been you and me, then all of a sudden Beth was there all the time, taking over. I hated it."

"She realizes she was wrong—we both do. Now I'm concerned about you."

"I've been behaving pretty badly," Samantha said.

"For understandable reasons. I haven't handled it well. I do care about Beth. I can't change that. But your feelings are important to me, too. Maybe we could all try again . . . start over."

Samantha hesitated. She still felt torn, but at least she knew now that her father wasn't trying to shut her out. Maybe Tor and Yvonne were right—her father deserved to have a woman in his life, if that was what he wanted. It didn't tarnish her mother's memory. "I'll try," she said, looking down at her hands. "I'm glad you talked to me, and I don't want Beth to think she has to leave because of me."

"She won't, but maybe it would be good for you and me to have some time together," Mr. McLean said. "It's not going to be an easy week leading up to the Whitney. You and Ashleigh are going to need some help sorting out this mess with the Townsends. I want to help you out all I can—without other distractions." He smiled sheepishly. "How about a hug?"

Beth had her suitcases packed and ready to go early the next morning. Samantha felt awkward, but she knew she had to say something to Beth before she left. Her father had gone to his room, leaving them alone.

Beth greeted Samantha with a smile. She didn't seem in the least angry, which made Samantha feel worse. "I haven't been very nice, have I?" Samantha said quickly.

"I know I've made things uncomfortable for you, but I don't want you to leave just because of me."

"I have felt pretty uncomfortable," Beth admitted, "but I think I understand where you were coming from, too. I know how hard it was for you to lose your mother. I should have been more considerate of your feelings and realized it would take you a while before you could accept another woman in your father's life. I think the world of your father and would like to be friends with you. Your father and I talked this morning. I've decided to head home anyway. You're both going to have a very busy week, and there are things I can get done at home. Maybe you and I could make a fresh start when you get back?"

Samantha nodded.

"I promise not to jump in with both feet again." Beth turned as Samantha's father came into the room.

"All set?" he asked. His question had a double meaning as he glanced back and forth between Beth and Samantha.

"I'm ready," Beth said with a smile.

Mr. McLean looked relieved. "I'll drop you at the track, Sammy, then take Beth to the airport limo. Tell Mike I'll be a few minutes late."

Ashleigh was already at Pride's stall when Samantha hurried up. Samantha glanced down the stabling row and saw that only Ken Maddock and Hank were outside the Townsend Acres stalls.

"They haven't gotten here yet," Ashleigh said. "But I'll have something to say to them when they do."

159

Samantha busied herself getting Pride ready for his workout. He whickered happily as she went into his stall. Samantha rubbed her hand over his sleek neck and smiled. "You look good this morning, fella. Ready to go out?" Pride snorted eagerly as Samantha removed his sheet and folded it, then reached for her brushes. She gave him a light grooming and cleaned his hooves, then clipped the lead shank to his halter and led him out. Len had already settled Pride's tack on the box outside the stall. Ashleigh gave Samantha a hand tacking him up.

"I want to clock him this morning," Ashleigh said as she tightened the girth.

"I see Brad and Lavinia still aren't here."

"I'm sure they'll show up. Maddock is working Lord Ainsley this morning."

Mike and Hank joined them, leading two of Mike's horses, and they all headed out to the track. Samantha repeated her father's message to Mike.

"I didn't realize Beth was leaving so soon," Mike said.

"She decided to head back early."

A number of horses were already out on the oval. Ken Maddock was giving Lord Ainsley's rider instructions, but there was still no sign of Lavinia and Brad.

Samantha concentrated her thoughts on the workout. She noticed that there were quite a few spectators and knew they had come because both Pride and Lord Ainsley were scheduled to work. The false rumor about Pride being scratched from the Whitney would have piqued interest, too.

Samantha settled herself in the saddle and headed

out to the track to put Pride through his warm-up paces. She noticed Lord Ainsley's rider was galloping him on the far side of the track.

Pride was moving beautifully. As they approached the mile marker pole Samantha clucked to him, and he took off in a ground-eating gallop. She held him to an easy gallop through the first half mile, then clucked again and gave rein, and Pride surged forward, breezing out the last half effortlessly.

He was still full of energy when Samantha pulled him up and headed off the track. "That's the way, big guy! But you hardly ever disappoint us, do you? Let's hope this makes Ashleigh feel a little better."

Samantha trotted him through the gap and was glad to see that Ashleigh was smiling. "Perfect, Sammy," she said as she held Pride so Samantha could dismount. "Couldn't be better."

"How did Lord Ainsley work?" Samantha asked.

"Unfortunately very good, too."

Samantha saw that her father had arrived—so had Lavinia and Brad. Mr. McLean walked over.

"So they're finally here," Ashleigh said, looking in the Townsends' direction. "I think I'll go over and have a little talk with them."

"Go on. I'll give Sammy a hand untacking Pride," Mr. McLean said.

Ashleigh strode determinedly a few yards down the rail to where Brad and Lavinia stood. Suddenly there was a hush in the crowd as the spectators strove to listen. Ashleigh made no attempt to lower her voice as she confronted Brad and Lavinia.

"A funny rumor is going around. I thought maybe you two know something about it."

"Oh, it *is* terrible, isn't it?" Lavinia said. "Brad and I have been doing what we can to stop it."

"Oh, get off it, Lavinia. You and Brad had to have started the rumor in the first place."

"That's nonsense," Brad said. "Don't make a fool out of yourself."

"No one would have believed the story if it hadn't come from a reliable source. It sure didn't come from me. Therefore, it had to have come from Townsend Acres, meaning you, since your father's in England."

Brad's voice was filled with scorn. "You really are making a fool out of yourself, Ashleigh."

"No, Brad, I think you've got that backward." Ashleigh turned and strode over to Samantha and Mr. McLean.

Lavinia gave an artificial laugh for the benefit of the spectators. "Imagine her thinking *we'd* start a rumor like that! And why is she letting such a silly thing upset her?"

Samantha saw a smile flicker on Ashleigh's lips as she walked up. "I figured they'd deny it," Ashleigh said, "but at least I got it off my chest."

14

FOR A WEEK ALL WAS CALM. SAMANTHA HAD THE HORRIBLE feeling that it was the lull before the storm and tried to convince herself that Ashleigh was right—Lavinia and Brad couldn't do much more to hurt them. The Whitney was in two days. Pride was in top form. Excitement was growing over the matchup of the top two handicap horses in the country.

"I wish I could stop worrying," Samantha said to Tor and Yvonne. Samantha had settled Pride in his stall for the afternoon, and they'd checked on Sierra. Mike had decided to race Sierra again during the last week of the meet.

"Why don't we get away from here for a while?" Tor suggested. "How about a walk into town? Take your mind off things."

"Sounds like a good idea to me," Yvonne said.

Samantha nodded. "You're right. I think I need to get away from here. Did Ashleigh tell you they're going to do a tribute to Charlie in the Paddock Pavilion before the race?"

"Yes, and I think it's great."

The walk into town did Samantha a world of good. She convinced herself she was worrying over nothing. The next days would go smoothly; Pride would be at his best and beat Lord Ainsley, and Ashleigh would have the satisfaction of triumphing over Lavinia and Brad.

Hank came up to them when they returned to the backside. "I got some bad news for you. Maddock just heard from Clay Townsend. He's going to be held up in England on business for some time. He won't be here for the race." Hank scowled. "Brad's in full charge until he gets back."

"Oh, no," Samantha said. "Have you told Ashleigh?"

"Yup. She, your father, and Mike are over in the lounge."

"Thanks, Hank. We'll go see her. Has Brad been around?"

"Nope. In fact, he and Lavinia have been laying low. Starting that rumor about Pride seems to have backfired on them. Anyway, haven't seen either one of them today."

Ashleigh was obviously upset over the new development. "I can't believe Mr. Townsend would do this to me. He must know that Brad and Lavinia can't be trusted."

"Brad's his son," Mr. McLean told her. "Parents are known to have a blind eye for their children's faults."

"Besides," Yvonne said, "they never try anything when he's around."

Mike reached across the table and squeezed Ashleigh's hand. "Nothing's happened yet. And if either of them do anything else to upset you, I'm not going to be a gentleman about it. Enough is enough."

"I agree with that," Mr. McLean said. He glanced over to Samantha and gave her a reassuring smile. For the last few days, they'd been getting along the way they used to. He talked to Beth every night, but Samantha wasn't as bothered now. She was seeing Beth as less of a threat. She wasn't entirely won over, though, either. She'd need more time to decide that, but she would try to make a fresh start once they got back home.

Everything continued to go smoothly through all of Friday. Lavinia and Brad showed up at Lord Ainsley's stall for a few minutes, then left the track.

"Have they said anything about the race?" Samantha asked Hank.

The groom shook his head. "Nothing except to say Lord looked ready to go. He had a really good workout this morning, and that made them happy."

Could it be possible they'd finally given up and wouldn't cause Ashleigh any more trouble? Samantha wondered.

Friday night they all went into town for dinner. Samantha noticed that Ashleigh only nibbled at her food. Samantha was getting a strong case of prerace jitters herself. After dinner they went back to the track to check on Pride. Len was seated on a camp chair outside the stall, enjoying the warm evening air.

"All's quiet," he told them. "I just checked Pride, and he's snoozing away."

Samantha and Ashleigh unhooked the top door and looked in. The beautiful chestnut horse was indeed dozing peacefully.

Mike put his arm around Ashleigh's shoulders. "I think it's time we went to bed, Ash. You look beat."

"I feel beat, but I don't know if I'm going to be able to sleep."

"It's time for all of us to turn in," Mr. McLean said. "Tor and Yvonne, I'll give you a lift to the motel." Now that Beth had left, Yvonne was staying with the McLeans. Tor had a room a few doors down.

Samantha tossed and turned for most of the night. She finally fell asleep for a few hours, but felt groggy as they all left for the track in the morning.

Ashleigh and Mike were already outside Pride's stall. The backside was humming with excitement. Several reporters appeared; others were gathered outside Lord Ainsley's stall talking to Ken Maddock. Samantha took Pride for a walk before things got much more hectic. Tor and Yvonne walked with her.

"So far, so good," Yvonne said. "I didn't see Lavinia or Brad here yet."

"No, but I'm sure they'll show up soon. They'd never miss a chance for publicity." Their absence, though, was making Samantha uneasy.

By ten o'clock Samantha had Pride bathed, groomed, and back in his stall. Tor had gone to check on Sierra and Yvonne to buy a *Daily Racing Form.*

Ashleigh came by to look Pride over. "He sure seems fine," she said after giving him a thorough inspection. "But I can't figure out where Jilly is. She said she was getting a red-eye special and would be here by now."

"Maybe her flight was delayed," Samantha said.

"Mmmm. Let me give the airport a call." Ashleigh hurried off.

A few minutes later a reporter came up to the stall. "I hear there's been a jockey change," he said to Samantha.

Samantha shook her head. "No. Jilly Gordon's riding."

"That's not what's on the morning record."

"They must have made a mistake. Jilly will be here." Even as she spoke, Samantha had a sinking feeling in her stomach.

"Somebody's got things screwed up," the reporter said, leaving in a huff.

Mike arrived to hear the end of the conversation. "What was that all about?" When Samantha explained, he frowned. "Where's Ashleigh?"

"Calling the airport. Jilly's flight must be late."

Ashleigh suddenly raced around the corner of the barn. "Mike," she cried. "I don't understand. I just called the airport. Jilly wasn't even listed on the flight. What's going on? Jilly would never let me down. She was looking forward to this race."

"Wait a minute," Mike said. "Just take it easy. Maybe she's on a different flight."

"But wouldn't she have called?"

"We didn't check at the motel desk for messages last night."

"Ashleigh," a voice called from behind them. "So I've finally tracked you down." They all turned to see Brad.

"What do you mean, tracked me down?" Ashleigh said. "I've been on the backside all morning."

"I was trying to get you last night. There was a problem. Jilly can't ride. I had to find a replacement, and since I couldn't reach you, I went ahead and lined up another jockey."

Ashleigh gasped. "What?"

"You wait until nearly eleven o'clock the morning of the race to tell us this?" Mike asked in amazement.

"I had some other appointments this morning," Brad replied. "This was the first chance I could get here."

"You could have found some way to notify her. And you can't just go assigning jockeys without Ashleigh's agreement."

"I didn't see that I had any options," Brad said mildly. "When I couldn't reach her last night, I didn't want to risk waiting until this morning. As it was, there weren't many replacement jockeys available. Most of them already had rides."

"So who did you get?" Ashleigh looked thunderous.

"Benny Alvero. He's been riding for Townsend Acres. Maddock and I have been happy with him."

"Benny Alvero?" Ashleigh cried in disbelief. "He's only ridden in a couple of races here, and I never heard of him before that!"

"Maybe not in this country, but he had plenty of experience in Mexico."

"Just how long has he been riding in the States?" Mike asked sharply.

Brad shrugged. "A few weeks. It's not a problem, though. He's ridden a couple of winners for Maddock already."

Samantha's head was spinning. Why would Jilly suddenly cancel without telling Ashleigh directly? She had a horrible feeling that there was more to the story than Brad was telling them. And for him to assign a nearly unknown jockey was a slap in Ashleigh's face. It was unthinkable.

"I want another jockey," Ashleigh said. "One of the top riders."

"A little late in the day for that," Brad said. "You're not going to find anyone else now. Of course, you could always scratch Pride."

Mike had balled his fists and looked ready to punch the smile off Brad's face. Ashleigh laid a restraining hand on his arm. Samantha shared Mike's anger, but she knew a fight would only make matters worse. Mike realized that, too, and visibly controlled himself.

"We won't be scratching Pride," Ashleigh told Brad. "I want to meet with Alvero."

"I'm sure Maddock can tell you where to find him. Well, I have other things to take care of this morning." Brad turned and stepped down the shed row.

Ashleigh's voice was laced with sarcasm as she called after him, "Thanks for all your help, Brad."

Brad continued walking as if he hadn't heard her.

"Darn them!" Mike said furiously. "If only there

was something *I* could do to help you out, Ash. I can't believe Jilly wouldn't have gotten in touch with you somehow."

"I'm going to call her. I can't believe it either. The thing that galls me is that I really don't have any option but to keep Alvero on. Brad knows I can't ride, not when I'm Pride's official trainer."

"Are you thinking that Lavinia and Brad will have Alvero deliberately lose the race?" Samantha asked.

"That would be illegal," Mike said. "But they sure can give the jockey their own set of instructions. Brad knows how Pride likes to run. He could tell Alvero to hold Pride way off the pace, which Pride would hate."

"The jockey's supposed to listen to the trainer," Samantha said.

"Sure," Ashleigh replied, "but Alvero's been riding for Townsend Acres, remember. Brad's been his boss. Let me try and call Jilly."

"I'll check for messages at the motel," Mike told her.

The next hours passed in a blur. Samantha stayed with Pride, trying to keep him as calm as possible as more people showed up wanting to know about the jockey change. Samantha fielded the questions as best she could. Tor and Yvonne were stunned by Brad and Lavinia's latest maneuver and kept Samantha company guarding the stall. Ashleigh couldn't reach Jilly on the phone but left a message on her answering machine telling Jilly to call her at the track. Mike returned from calling the motel with the news that Jilly

170

had called twice the night before, leaving a message at the front desk that it was urgent Ashleigh get back to her.

"And we didn't check at the front desk. We were too tired," Ashleigh said with a frown. "Now I'm really worried, though. Something must have happened."

"There weren't any messages at the desk from Brad, though," Mike added angrily. "It looks like he assigned Alvero without even trying to reach you."

Somehow, Samantha wasn't surprised.

Mr. McLean and Len came by when they had finished settling the Whitebrook horses. "Have you talked to Maddock?" Mr. McLean asked Ashleigh.

"Yup. Brad didn't tell him anything about the jockey change until this morning. Maddock said Alvero is a decent enough rider, but he'd be better for more experience. Maddock couldn't believe Brad had put him up on Pride. Brad's explanation to Maddock was that he wanted to give Alvero a chance."

"And try to ruin Pride's chances in the process," Samantha replied grimly.

Ashleigh sighed. "Brad would never have tried this on Charlie. He's really taking advantage of me, isn't he?"

"Don't get down on yourself," Mike told her. "Make sure your instructions are clear to Alvero in the walking ring. You know Pride is ready to race, and you can count on him putting in his best effort."

A few minutes later Ashleigh finally received a call from Jilly, from California. She hurried off to the trainers' office to answer it. When she returned a few

171

minutes later, she was looking bleak.

"Jilly just got the message I left on her machine," Ashleigh said. "She was at the hospital. Craig was involved in a spill at Del Mar yesterday afternoon. They thought he was all right, but when Jilly was getting ready to leave for the airport to come here, Craig passed out." The others gasped, but Ashleigh quickly continued. "Jilly rushed him to the hospital and tried to call me. When I didn't return her calls, as a last resort she called the track stewards' office and told them to get word to me that she couldn't ride. The stewards must have notified Brad instead, thinking he'd pass the message on to me." Ashleigh scowled.

"Jilly is sick over what happened. She's sure we could have gotten one of the top jockeys if we'd contacted them last night."

"How's Craig?" Samantha asked.

"Thankfully, he's going to be okay. It looks like he only had a slight concussion, but they're keeping him at the hospital for observation."

"You're going to say something to Brad, aren't you?" Mr. McLean asked.

"You bet I am. Though with only two hours until the race goes off, it's too late to change things."

15

THE CROWD WAS SIX DEEP ALONG THE FENCE SURROUNDING the tree-shaded saddling paddock as the field was readied for the Whitney. Many in the crowd had come from viewing the tribute to Charlie, and Samantha noticed a few misty eyes. She heard comments, too, as she walked Pride around the ring after Ashleigh had saddled him.

"Charlie Burke will be rolling in his grave after this race. What the heck is the Griffen girl thinking of, putting up Alvero?"

Samantha was glad Ashleigh wasn't listening. The jockey change was affecting the handicappers' opinions, too. Lord Ainsley was now considered the favorite, although, since he and Pride were running as an entry, their odds were the same. And there had been a late entry in the field—Super Value, a horse who had beaten Pride the year before. Super Value had been sidelined for nine months, but Samantha knew he could pose a real threat, particularly if Alvero didn't ride the race the way Ashleigh instructed.

Samantha saw Brad and Lavinia standing by Lord Ainsley's saddling box, both of them looking very smug, like cats licking their lips. Ashleigh had confronted Brad. He had sworn up and down that he had tried to call her but there was no answer in her room. Unfortunately, no one could prove otherwise.

Ashleigh joined Samantha and Pride as the jockeys entered the ring and went to their respective mounts. Samantha was immediately struck by Alvero's youth—but that didn't necessarily mean anything. Jilly and Ashleigh were young, too, and both had won plenty of races. But when Ashleigh started giving the jockey firm instructions, Samantha really began to worry. At first the jockey didn't seem to be listening, then he mumbled something in such heavily accented English that neither Ashleigh nor Samantha could understand him. Samantha wondered if he was even speaking English. She wished Yvonne were in the ring. She would have understood.

"Keep him *on* or close to the lead," Ashleigh reemphasized. "Let him out at the head of the stretch. When he changes leads, he'll really accelerate."

Samantha glanced at Pride. He seemed confused to have a strange rider on his back. He snorted uneasily, and Samantha quietly soothed him. "It'll be okay, boy," she whispered. "Jilly couldn't ride, but you can do it even with a different jock. Go out and win it for Ashleigh . . . and for Charlie." She dropped a kiss on his nose as she always did before he raced. "I believe in you, boy."

Pride huffed softly. Samantha circled Pride with Alvero on his back, then Alvero tightened his grip on the reins as the field filed toward the fenced lane that led to the track. Samantha gave Pride a last pat, then stepped away as the jockeys and horses moved forward.

Ashleigh came up beside her. "Here's hoping," she said. Then they hurried to the clubhouse with Mike, Mr. McLean, Tor, and Yvonne. Tor sat beside Samantha and laid his hand on her knee.

"What do you think of the jockey?" he asked with concern.

"That he didn't understand half of what Ashleigh was saying, and if he did understand, he wasn't listening."

"I was afraid of that."

"And I don't think he's been riding in this country long enough to know Pride's history or racing style," Samantha said.

The field was starting to load into the gate. The crowd was restless with excitement. Samantha hated to see Alvero in Pride's saddle, and Pride still seemed uneasy with the new rider. He fidgeted as the ten-horse field finished loading.

Then the gate doors snapped open. Within two strides of the gate Samantha could see that Alvero definitely was following instructions other than Ashleigh's. She cursed under her breath to see Alvero choking Pride back as he tried to hold the big horse off the pace. The rest of the field was out smartly, leaving Pride in its wake. Lord Ainsley was settled in off the leaders, just where he liked to be. And there was Pride at the back of the pack, his neck arched as he fought the pressure on his reins and tried to run freely.

"Costar has taken the early lead," the announcer cried, "then Orbital; Lord Ainsley is just behind them. Phone Line in fourth, then Mari's Pleasure, Redeemable, White Cross, Super Value. As they head to the clubhouse turn, Wonder's Pride is trailing the field. He's *ten lengths* off the pace!" The announcer sounded mystified. Samantha wasn't surprised.

Tor took her hand and squeezed it. Samantha felt sick watching her beloved horse being made to lose the race. She could almost feel Pride's confusion as he received signals that were totally different from those he'd received in the past. Samantha heard Ashleigh's groan, and glancing over saw that she was white faced with anger.

Lord Ainsley was running beautifully, set to make his move on the far turn. As the field moved down the backstretch Pride was still ten lengths behind and still fighting for rein. Samantha was afraid that even when Alvero finally gave Pride rein, Pride would be so unsettled and confused, he would just stop trying.

Samantha wanted to scream. She wanted to wring Lavinia and Brad's necks for giving Alvero instructions that could ultimately hurt Pride. Alvero's ride could cost Pride more than just the race. The big chestnut was struggling so hard to get rein and go after the rest of the field, it was very possible he would come out of the race a physical mess.

"They're going to ruin him!" Samantha cried to Tor. He tightened his grip on her hand and stared grimly at the track, obviously sharing her fears.

The field was entering the far turn, with Pride far back. And Alvero showed no signs of releasing his choking hold.

"Lord Ainsley is starting to make his move," the announcer called. "As they go into the far turn, he's moving up outside of Costar and Orbital. Phone Line is holding on in fourth, then Redeemable, Mari's Pleasure . . . but Super Value is moving now, too, splitting horses and gaining in midpack! Wonder's Pride still ten lengths off the pace! He's not running in his style at all. This definitely isn't one of his better days."

Samantha groaned again. From the crowd nearby she heard a fan cry out angrily, "What's that Griffen girl thinking of, running him like this! She's out of her mind!"

Ashleigh must have heard, too, and Samantha felt wrenching sympathy for her friend. Ashleigh was being blamed for Lavinia and Brad's irresponsible actions.

Then Samantha gasped. Pride had had enough of Alvero's hold. Just when Samantha was sure all was lost, Pride forcefully thrust his magnificent head forward. He wrenched the reins through Alvero's fingers and grabbed the bit. Samantha let out a yelp of joy as Pride, finally able to run freely, leaped ahead with powerful strides as if he'd been shot from a cannon.

Suddenly the announcer's voice brimmed with excitement. "Here comes Wonder's Pride! Flying up the track. He's closing with every stride. As they head out of the far turn, Lord Ainsley easily puts away Costar and Orbital, but Wonder's Pride is coming on strong! So is Super Value. Here's the horse race we've been waiting for!"

The crowd seemed to expel a united breath of relief and awe. Pride was passing horses like they were standing still. Samantha knew what Pride was capable of, but even to her eyes, his burst of speed was incredible. The crowd roared their encouragement and approval. They loved what they were seeing.

Pride was four wide coming out of the far turn, and he was still effortlessly passing horses. Alvero was no more than a passenger on his back. But Lord Ainsley was still several lengths in the lead, and Super Value was moving up through the center of the pack.

"Come on, Pride!" Samantha screamed as Pride powered out of the turn and shot forward with another burst of speed. Lord Ainsley's jockey never looked back to see if anyone was challenging him. He must have been confident that Pride wouldn't be a threat. "Won't Le Blanc be surprised," Samantha murmured to Tor with dour satisfaction.

"At the sixteenth pole, Lord Ainsley has a two-length lead!" the announcer cried. "Wonder's Pride is roaring up on his outside. Wonder's Pride shoots by on the outside! The big chestnut has the lead and is drawing off! Le Blanc goes to his whip. Alvero seems to be hanging on for the ride. Super Value moves up into a fast-closing third! They're coming down to the finish! Lord Ainsley is running gamely, giving chase, but Wonder's Pride is lengthening his lead! They're under the wire! It's Wonder's Pride by two lengths *going away*! Then Lord Ainsley, Super Value another length back in third. The rest far behind. After a mystifying start, Wonder's Pride has put in an amazing performance and finishes brilliantly!"

They were all on their feet and cheering. "Did you ever see anything like it?" Samantha cried.

"No!" Ashleigh said, nearly beside herself with excitement. "I can hardly believe it. After all Lavinia and Brad put him through, he still beat their horse! I can't *wait* to see their faces."

"I just hope the effort he had to put in didn't take too much out of him," Mike said.

They all rushed down through the stands. An outrider joined Alvero and Pride, and they trotted toward the winner's circle. Alvero's expression was hard to read, but he seemed dazed.

Worried about Pride's condition, Samantha hurried to collect him from the outrider. Ashleigh and Mike were right behind her. Pride was blowing hard after his effort, and his copper coat was lathered in sweat. Samantha felt an anxious knot in her stomach as she led Pride forward. Ashleigh and Mike were carefully studying his movements, too. Drenched in sweat though he was, Pride seemed to be walking freely and comfortably. He wasn't favoring his previously injured foreleg, which had been Samantha's greatest fear. But after the performance he had put in, especially after the stress of being held against his

179

will, Samantha knew Pride had to be absolutely exhausted. Again she felt the urge to wring Lavinia and Brad's necks!

She took Pride's head and gently caressed his nose as she, Ashleigh, and Mike led Pride into the winner's circle. Tired as he was, Pride held his head high and pricked his ears at the cheering crowd. Samantha felt her heart swell at his courage. She noticed Alvero was scowling as he dismounted and started removing the saddle to weigh in. He mumbled several angry sentences. Neither Ashleigh nor Samantha could understand, but Yvonne had come up beside them, and as Alvero strode off, Yvonne translated. "He said, 'Why did they tell me to hold him off the pace? I could have ruined him. It's crazy!'"

"That comment gives me a little ammunition," Ashleigh said grimly. The crowd was gathering around the winner's circle, which at Saratoga was literally a chalk circle drawn on the track. Samantha gently stroked Pride's neck. "You did an absolutely incredible job today, boy. I'm *so* proud of you! You showed them!"

Pride whickered his thanks. He was still breathing hard, and Samantha frowned for a moment in worry. She would give him very special treatment when they got back to the barn—a cooling bath and a long walk and massage, and a bran mash for his dinner.

Alvero returned, and Pride was resaddled for the winner's photo as Lavinia and Brad strode into the ring. Lavinia's look to Ashleigh was lethal.

Ashleigh spoke just loudly enough so that Lavinia

and Brad could hear her. "I think we have something to discuss after we leave the winner's circle," she said. "It might even be a matter for the stewards—a little thing called race fixing?"

Samantha saw that for once Lavinia's haughty confidence seemed to be shaken. But Lavinia quickly pasted a smile on her lips as a television cameraman aimed in her direction. She stepped over to Pride's head. Samantha gritted her teeth as she watched Lavinia primp for the camera. Then Pride did something Samantha had never seen him do before. As Lavinia approached, he flattened his ears and bared his teeth in menacing warning.

Lavinia jumped back in horror. Her phony smile turned to a comical look of fright. Samantha could barely stop herself from laughing. "Good boy," she whispered to Pride.

Brad strode over quickly and took Lavinia's arm. He made a pretense of soothing her ruffled nerves. "Let's go," he said. "After that, I don't particularly want to be in this photo."

"See you later for our little talk," Ashleigh said cheerfully. Then she took her place at Pride's head beside Samantha. She raised her voice for the benefit of the onlookers. "Earlier this afternoon," she said, "the Saratoga track graciously hosted a memorial tribute to a wonderful man and dedicated trainer, Charlie Burke. He taught me everything I know. I have Charlie to thank for Pride's success, and by his winning today's race, I think Pride has proved himself to be a true champion. That's the best tribute of all to Charlie and

181

his wisdom and his talent. We're going to miss you, Charlie!"

Samantha laid her cheek against Pride's head, and when the crowd applauded wildly, she smiled through the mist of tears in her eyes. She knew that if Charlie was watching, he was smiling, too—and not just because of Pride's magnificent victory. At last Ashleigh had come out on top, in spite of Lavinia and Brad's best efforts!

About the Author

Joanna Campbell, born and raised in Norwalk, Connecticut, grew up loving horses, and eventually owned a horse of her own. She took riding lessons for a number of years, and specialized in open jumping. She has published twenty novels for young adults, sung and played piano professionally, and owned an antique business. She now lives on the coast of Maine with her husband, Ian, and her two children, Kimberly and Kenneth.

THOROUGHBRED

✦✦✦✦✦✦✦✦✦✦✦✦✦✦✦✦✦✦✦✦✦✦✦✦✦✦✦✦✦✦✦✦✦✦✦✦✦✦

If you enjoyed this book, then you'll love reading all the books in the THOROUGHBRED series!

✦✦✦✦✦✦✦✦✦✦✦✦✦✦✦✦✦✦✦✦✦✦✦✦✦✦✦✦✦✦✦✦✦✦✦✦✦✦

**At bookstores everywhere,
or call 1-800-331-3761 to order.**

HarperCollins*Publishers*
www.harpercollins.com

THOROUGHBRED

**All books are
$4.50 U.S./$5.50 Canadian**

Whoa—There's a Whole New Series
Coming Your Way, Starring Thoroughbred's
Best-loved Character, Ashleigh Griffen!

Introducing Ashleigh,
the new series from Joanna Campbell. . . .

Lightning's Last Hope
Ashleigh #1
ISBN 0-06-106540-4
$4.50/$5.50 (Can.)

A Horse For Christmas
Ashleigh #2
ISBN 0-06-106542-0
$4.50/$5.50 (Can.)

And look for these upcoming titles:

Available in
February!

Waiting For Stardust
Ashleigh #3
ISBN 0-06-106544-7

**Goodbye,
Midnight Wanderer**
Ashleigh #4
ISBN 0-06-106557-9

Available in
April!

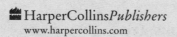

HarperCollins*Publishers*
www.harpercollins.com

At bookstores
everywhere, or call
1-800-331-3761 to order.